Watch out, HOLLYWOOD!
MORE Confessions of a So-called
Middle Child

Watch out, HOLLYWOOD! MORE Confessions of a So-called Middle Child

by Maria T. Lennon

HARPER

An Imprint of HarperCollinsPublishers

Library of Congress Cataloging-in-Publication Data
Lennon, M. T. (Maria T.)
    Watch out, Hollywood! / by Maria T. Lennon. — First edition.
        pages   cm
    Sequel to: Confessions of a so-called middle child.
    Summary: The trials and tribulations of twelve-year-old Charlie C. Cooper,
reformed bully, gifted hacker, and middle child, continue as Charlie tries to convert her
overnight fame into a lucrative role on a television show.
    ISBN 978-0-06-212694-8
    [1. Fame—Fiction. 2. Friendship—Fiction. 3. Middle-born children—
Fiction. 4. Middle schools—Fiction. 5. Schools—Fiction. 6. Los Angeles
(Calif.)—Fiction. 7. Humorous stories.] I. Title.
PZ7.L53935 Wat 2014   2013043139
[Fic]—dc23   CIP
                                                                                    AC

Typography by Michelle Gengaro-Kokmen
15 16 17 18 19   CG/OPM   10 9 8 7 6 5 4 3 2 1
❖
First paperback edition, 2015

To my absolutely gorgeous mom and dearly missed dad; my amazing sister, Susan; hysterically funny brothers, Patrick and George—if I could have picked a family, I could not have picked a better one than you. Quite simply, you are the best family a girl could ask for.

To my husband, Davide, thank you, thank you for letting me do what I love to do. To our beautiful children, Chiara, Lucia, Pablo, and Rocco, watching you have each other's backs makes me prouder than just about anything. I hope one day you'll grow up and feel the same way about your siblings and parents as I do about mine. Pure love.

Watch out, HOLLYWOOD! MORE Confessions* of a So-called Middle Child

Nirvana, Baby

Here's why I believe in second chances:

Yesterday, I was running for my life. Hiding from the cops. Everyone hated me. It was over. Everything I'd hoped for. And I'm not lying. If there's one thing you should know about me, Charlie C. Cooper, I don't lie. I might be a lot of things, but I'm no liar.

Anyway, as I was saying, there I was hiding in the Houdini tunnels with Marta the Farta like a dirty rat while the police and Principal Pickler hunted us down like dogs.

And today I am a hero. No joke. My face is literally splashed all over the TV.

You're probably asking yourselves how could a super cool,

smart, fashion forward, tech genius such as myself be hunted down like a rat?

Well, I'll tell you. It's because my no-good, super jealous and totally spoiled ex-friend Trixie wanted us gone. She wanted Marta off the school gym team and me off the planet Earth. And she's the kind of girl who will do whatever it takes to get what she wants. So when she found out the secret we'd been hiding—that Marta's mom was really dead and she was living alone—she called the cops, Social Services, and, of course, Principal Pickler. And it looked like she was going to get her way too, until my last-minute plan worked and Marta's aunt arrived from Romania to take care of her. Trixie got kicked out. Her sidekick Babette got a big fat dose of therapy. And me—I was off the hook. I was also off the couch and out of the doghouse. No more therapy for this girl. I was cured in the eyes of the world.

The press got hold of the story and ran with it. Love those guys.

And here we are. One day after the whole thing went down and I'm waking up to a wall of lightbulbs and cameras lined up along the fence outside my house calling my name, chanting it like a roar.

"*Charlie!*"

"*Charlie!*"

"*Charlie!*"

Okay, fine. They aren't really chanting, but you get my drift, right? They're waiting. For me. Charlie. And I am so

2

ready. I put together an outfit no one will forget.

My signature blue Dr. Martens, fishnet tights, black tutu, and, of course, my Guns N' Roses vintage sweatshirt with faux sweat rings. I tease the hair, stick tons of black butterfly sequin barrettes in, put a tiny bit of my sister's mascara on, and *bam!* A star is about to be born.

There's a knock at the front door. I run to answer it.

"Yo! Charlie! CNN." They snap my picture. "*LA Times*. Over here, Charlie!"

"*People* magazine," someone yells. "Can you tell our readers what it feels like to be a hero?"

"A hero?" Now that's a first.

"Show us where it happened, Charlie."

"ABC here," a camera with the biggest microphone ever is suddenly in my face, "is it really true you found Houdini's lost tunnels?"

I take the key from my pocket. "Follow me."

The TV people call me selfless. They call me a true friend. They say I risked my life to help Marta, whose mom had died. Finally I'm being seen for the person I want to be *instead* of the person I was. A bully, yeah that's right. I can admit it now. I, Charlie C. Cooper was a bully. But those days are gone. And lucky for me, Chad Newman, my major agent from Endeavor, is by my side, reminding me of the bright spot at the end of the tunnel. "We're gonna make you a star, Charlie Cooper, a star."

After the press conference, right around lunchtime, Chad

announces that we have offers on the table from ABC Family, Nick, and possibly even HBO, all begging to sign me. By Sunday morning, my face is plastered across every paper in LA with the headlines: Ex-bully, Turned Selfless Do-gooder, Charlie C. Cooper Used Her Hacking Skills to Save the Poor, Bullied Orphan Marta the Farta and Find the Houdini Tunnels. All in one night! CNN runs the story so much that even my good friend Jai hears about it in Mumbai. By four in the afternoon, I've got boxes of thick, gooey salted caramels stacked on my doorstep with notes from Hollywood agents begging to turn me into a household name. But I'm taken. I've signed with Chad. And if there's one thing you should know about me it's that I'm as loyal as the school day is long.

Now I can almost bet that come Monday morning, I will be the most popular kid in Happy Canyon School. And we're not talking empty popularity, like the girls who are popular because their boobs are bigger than most of the moms' or because their dads drive cars that cost more than a house. I'm talking *sustainable popularity*. My Indian friend Jai says it's the only kind of popularity that means anything, because it *means* something. I have no idea what exactly, but who cares, right? All that pain and suffering has finally paid off.

To go with my new self, I need a new outfit, of course—

"Charlie?" Mom calls up from the kitchen. "Chad's on the phone. He sounds crazed."

I throw on my Led Zeppelin tank top, black skirt, and

boots, and am about to walk out, when I hear Felix in the hallway, bouncing off the walls. "Charlie's gonna be famous, Charlie's gonna be famous."

I'm feeling warm and fuzzy all over.

"Charlie! Get down here now!" Mom yells again.

Then my older sister, Penelope, the do-gooder, throws open my door. "Exploitation is so lame. And you, my little sister, are being exploited."

For some reason she's always right there, just waiting to yuck my yum. "Can you move, please?"

"No."

Sadly, it's their room too. So embarrassing. The three of us—as in THREE—share one room, which I'm pretty sure is against the Geneva Convention. The next mansion that Dad gets hired to restore better have five bedrooms, or I'm out.

"Get a life, Pen." I pop one last delicious raspberry-filled See's candy on my tongue and suck the filling right out. "Here, kid." I hand Felix a chocolate, push Pen out of the way with one finger, and take the stairs fast and hard.

I grab the phone, feeling confident and ready for whatever else my wonderful life wants to toss my way, and run back up to the bathroom for some privacy. "Hey, Chad, what's happening?" Did I mention that Chad's from William Morris Endeavor? WME for those in the know? He represents the best of the best. People with last names like Cruz and Pitt. He's got more teeth than a shark, and his eyelids didn't close once during our meeting yesterday. A very good sign.

"Hey, star." Chad is smooth as silk. "Just heard ABC Family is casting for a new show called *Off the Beam.*

"Great title, don't you think? It's about a perfect team of girls who will do whatever it takes to be the best."

Sounds like middle school.

"And then there's the one kid who can't get on the team, the girl they all laugh at, pick on. That's you."

I'm speechless.

"Charlie, it's a great role. This kid is funny and smart, but she's a troublemaker. She's the star of the show."

Hold on. "Did you say star?"

"I did.

"You ever watch that show *Make It or Break It?*"

"I don't watch TV. I stream French movies."

"Well, it's a show about a group of gymnasts who all want to be the best on the team and they'll do anything to get there. They're ruthless." He says it like a yummy dessert. "It's like watching a bunch of cute kittens in pink leotards clawing each other's eyes out.

"You'd play the little sister villain. You know, messing up their hair, putting food coloring in their shampoo, that kind of stuff."

"Pranks?" Are you kidding me? I basically wouldn't have to act. "I would be perfect. Perfect! Where do I sign?"

"Hold on." He yanks me back from my moment of true happiness. "If you don't know the basics of gymnastics, they aren't interested."

What? All you need to do is look at me to know it ain't happening. I lift my tank top, stand sideways, and check out the tummy in the mirror. Not exactly gymnast material. I suck it in, basically stop breathing. Better.

"They want your friend to come in, too. She's good at gymnastics, right?"

"Whoa, wait, what friend? I don't have any friends."

He thinks this is hysterical. "The girl you hid in the tunnels. Got the aunt on a plane, you know . . . what's her name, kinda weird looking—"

"Marta." I close my eyes with a feeling of dread. Not Marta.

TRUE FACT: Can't this be about me, just me, for once?

"Exactly." He snaps. "What's her number?"

No, no, no! I pace my floor. I look out at my statue of Harry. "Charlie?"

My future passes in front of my eyes. It's the old fork in the road, people. If I don't give him her number, I see:

- ME, as the star of the show. Limo and driver, people kissing my butt, cameras following my every move.

But if I tell him the truth and give it to him, I see:

- Marta taking over as star gymnast on *my* new hit show, wanted by both Hollywood and the US Olympic team.
- Her teeth bleached and her clothes covered in rhinestones. Loved and adored by all.
- And ME, forgotten as usual.

I look at Houdini. He's looking right back at me. What would he do? What would Mr. Harry Houdini do? I pause, I pace, I really think about it. But the answer is obvious. Of course he'd do it. Of course he'd lie. And let's be honest, it's not really a lie, 'cause like I said, I'm no liar. It's more of a white lie. And who doesn't white lie? White lies are as common as words—like when people ask you how you're doing and you say, Fine, when you're not fine, that's a white lie. This town is built on them.

"I need your friend's number." Chad's pushing hard. "They want to see her just in case, as a backup. You know what I mean?"

Once again, the two versions of my life pass before my eyes. If they see Marta and me together, they'll choose her.

"Come on, kid, don't have all day," Chad barks.

And then I do it.

I lie.

Not a big lie.

Not a lie that will hurt anyone.

Just a small little lie that will help me. ME, Charlie.

I deserve a little help sometimes too, don't I?

Don't I?

I clear my throat. "I didn't want to say this because she's my best friend—"

"Go ahead," he says eagerly, like I'm about to drop a juicy piece of gossip.

"Marta's got issues."

"We all got issues, kid." He laughs. "Her number, please."

I go to the window and blow against it until I can't see out. I close my eyes.

I'm doing her a favor.

I'm doing her a favor.

I'm doing her a favor.

"Her mom just died."

"Great. She needs cash."

"No!" I stammer. "She's a nut job, doesn't shower, barely leaves the house. She's unstable and hates Hollywood."

He jumps in. "Whoa! Fine. I get it. She's psycho."

There. I did it. I take a deep breath. I feel a little sick. I'm gonna make it up to her, I will, I swear on my—

"It's all you, kid. And you're gonna be huge."

"Huge?" I'm shaking, but things are looking better.

"What kid who's a little overweight, a little uncoordinated and lost won't relate—"

"Hold up." Now he's going too far. I'm about to get a little ticked off when I hear three magic words . . .

"It's a series, Charlie." He lets that little delectable morsel of info fall just like that.

TRUE FACT: I will miss years of school.

"And that means a lot of money." He sounds like the cat who's just eaten the canary.

I stare at my reflection in the mirror and I ask, "Like, how much money?"

Now, before you go judging me, let me ask you a question: Have you seen the latest copy of *People* magazine? Well, I have. I know what happens to kids in Hollywood. They drop like flies. Like flies, I tell you. They're in one day and out the next. Gone for good. And I, Charlie C. Cooper, am not going down like that. No way. I gotta shoot high. Make it while I can.

"If it does well, we're talking movies, clothing lines, record deals, perfume—"

What? Did he say perfume? "Can we call it 'Charlie'?"

"The sky's the limit, kid. The producers want to capitalize on you, Charlie. They think you speak to kids all over the world. An ex-bully who put herself on the line for that kid."

"What kid?"

He laughs. "You're funny, too."

Oh, that kid. "Yep. Totally put my life on the line for her. Where do I sign?"

10

"Hold up." He laughs like I'm kidding. "You gotta audition."

"Audition?" Say what?

"And you'll need to send over your head shots."

"Head shots?" This is getting complicated.

"You don't have them? Who doesn't have head shots in LA?" he says. "No worries. There's a guy on Sunset I use all the time. Tell him I sent you. You're their first choice."

"Really?"

"Yep, you got what it takes, kid—I can see it," he says. "If you want it badly enough, you'll go far. You got a pen?"

I write the number down. "How much does it cost?"

"About five hundred bucks." He says it like five hundred bucks is pocket change.

I choke. "Five hundred bucks?"

Another reason to keep Marta away. She could never afford this. And plus, she'd hate it.

TRUE FACT: The more I think about it, I'm actually doing Marta a favor.

I race up the ladder to Pen's bed, reach under her mattress, and find her wallet. Pen usually has some major cash because of all those do-gooder tutoring jobs she does. I open it, and my heart falls. Ten bucks? Seriously?

"When do you think you can come in and show them what you got?"

My stomach cramps up. "Um . . ." I need time. Like a year. The last time I stretched I was seven.

"I'll give you till Friday to put together a great routine and get the head shots. Sound good? I'll send someone to pick you up."

A week? I pace my room. I glance at myself in the mirror. How am I ever going to come up with a routine and that kind of cash in a week?

Wait a sec—

"Will it be a limo with a pool? You'll pick me up at school, right? Oh, man, I need you to pick me up at school."

He laughs. "Already thinking like a star. You just might make it in this town. See you Friday." He hangs up.

One week. Not even Mandela or Jobs could become a pro gymnast in one week. I run to the window and crank it open. "Moooooom!"

Mom stops digging and looks up at me with a shovel in her hand. My parents are a real team. While Dad rebuilds the original Houdini mansion, Mom landscapes the gardens.

I lean out the window and whisper, "Do you believe in me, Mom?"

She smiles proudly. "Of course I believe in you."

I take a deep breath. "Great! Do you think you could loan me five hundred bucks?"

She laughs.

"For the head shots that will one day make millions."

"That's a lot of money, Charlie," she says. She goes back to digging like I'm just fooling around.

I run down the stairs and out into the garden. I take the shovel from her hands and try to impress upon her that without the investment we, as a family, are dead in the water. "Soon Dad's gonna be done with this project and we're not going to have any money coming in—"

She tries to take the shovel back. "You're twelve."

"But if I get a part in this new TV series that Chad wants me to audition for, then maybe we could buy this place ourselves. What do you say?"

"That's very sweet of you to think of us, but Charlie, you're going to have to earn that money. I won't give it to you."

Did she say earn? "But how? After I got busted for the prank masterpiece of all time and got kicked out of school, I swore on my life that I wouldn't hack anymore, which leaves me with zero earning power."

She starts digging, then stops. "How about the Pumpkin Patch on Sunset? I think they're looking for volunteers this Halloween. The tips are supposed to be great."

"*The* Pumpkin Patch?" As in the place kids from school go to be seen in their coolest outfits?

"Work there for a week, do a good job, and I'll make sure you have enough for your head shots."

A week of work? Oh, Mandela, help! A week of enslavement? Of forced labor? Of total humiliation?

"We'll go and talk to the owners." She smiles. "It'll be fun."

"Fun?" You gotta be kidding me.

But then I remember:

The path to fame is lined with the bodies of the weak. I, Charlie C. Cooper, am not weak. I, Charlie C. Cooper am ready to sacrifice— My computer rings. I click on the screen. It's Jai, my friend from India. The problem with Jai is that he can see into my soul. I hit ignore as fast as I can.

Fame Is Better Than Chicken Nuggets and Ranch

So we're walking to school the next morning, Pen is teaching Felix some "life lesson," and all I can think about is that if I play my cards right, I will:

- Have my very own TV series.
- Car and driver.
- Paparazzi following my every move.
- Huge Twitter following.
- Get Bobby to really like me, as in *sustainable* like— as in get dropped off by the parents and hang out at the Grove Mall like.

I'm so full of hope—which is rare for me—I don't even realize how far I've walked until I see my old enemy Principal Pickler in the parking lot, and all that positivity just drains from my heart. He's wearing a bad suit and a freakish grin like he wants something. Pickler always wants something.

"Hello, Cooper." He puts out his hand. "I'll admit I was wrong about you."

I shake it, even though I seriously don't want to.

It's the first time I've seen him since that night he came to our house with the cops and Social Services.

Pickler puts his long skinny arm around me and grins like the Joker. "Why don't you come to my office for a little visit?"

In the old days, I'd be sweating, trying to figure out what I was about to get busted for. But not anymore.

Pen taps him on his shoulder. "If you have a moment, I'd like to talk to you about what's happening in the canyons."

He looks totally confused. "What's happening, exactly?"

"Well, sir, those new megamansions that are being built up on Stanley Hills are killing the animals. You're aware that it's called the wildlife corridor because that's where the animals pass through the hills, aren't you?"

"Uh . . ." He shakes his head, points to his office. "I'll have to get back to you on that."

TRUE FACT: That's his line whenever he doesn't want to answer the question.

16

If Pen actually thinks Pickler cares more about the squirrels than the mansions, it makes me wonder what "gifted" really means. Felix, meanwhile, hopeless as ever, has found a dead rose and is trying to replant it.

"Charlie, shall we?" He points to his office.

I follow him into his little office. He points at the chair. "Sit, please."

I look at the clock on the wall. It's already past eight, which means my homeroom teacher, Mr. Lawson—Mr. L for short—has already started on his Gratitude Prayer.

I hate the Gratitude Prayer.

If I'm lucky, I'll miss the whole thing, and then tomorrow I can talk about being grateful for having missed the dumb gratitude speech. Knock out two days at once. Yippee.

Pickler leans forward and peels off a really long, gross cuticle. "I saw you on TV last night. Ex-bully turned selfless do-gooder."

"That's me." I beam. I like this new role.

Pickler narrows his eyes. "So you and Marta are tight?"

"Yeah." I look away.

He leans back. The chair squeaks. "Did you know the Junior Olympics are coming up in two weeks?"

"Say what?" I ask calmly, but inside I am screaming! Yes, screaming! Fate is so clearly on my side, it isn't even funny. If I can get her into the Junior Olympics, my lie is canceled. Slate wiped clean. Once again, Charlie = Hero.

"This is the most important competition of the year for Happy Canyon. This is where we get ninety percent of our donations, where we recruit our top athletes, our prestigious teachers. Where we get all of our press." Pickler practically screams. Then he opens his desk and pulls out the program sheet. "We need Marta there. We have to have her there. Can you help me?"

"Help you?" I jump out of my chair. "Marta would sell her left kidney to go—"

He points to the chair. "It's not that easy."

"Why?"

"The aunt refuses to pay. I've been on the phone with her all weekend, and she's refusing to pay a cent. Not a single cent. Did I mention it's in Texas? We're talking hotels, food, transportation, and fees." He puts his feet up on the desk. "I don't know what to do."

I hear screaming outside. I get up and look out his small window, even though I know who's causing the pain. It's Marta, all right, and she's back to wearing her signature homeless Disney princess look—pink velour bottoms, pink crocs, and socks. Her hair and face look like she's never met a mirror in her life. And she's got a mood to match. Dragging that dirty old pink Disney princess backpack over the feet of anyone in her way. They cry out. I can hear her yelling at them as her wheels run over their feet. "Move your dumb feet!"

"You gotta get her in the JOs." I smile at the sight of her. "She'll take the team all the way."

18

"Of course she'll take the team all the way," he yells like a crazy person. "But her aunt won't pay." Pickler slaps his desk. "Everyone pays their own way—this isn't the Goodwill, you know. It's a public school."

"They're broke."

"Who isn't?" Pickler counters. "Look, if we pay for her, then we'll have to pay for everyone. The board will never allow it. You have to get them to pay. My hands are tied."

"Untie them." I walk over to his desk and whisper, "Harvard Westlake's been calling."

All color drains from his face. "What? No! Not Harvard Westlake!"

"I'd pay for Marta before they snap her up for a full scholarship."

"But, but . . ." Spit foams at the corners of his mouth. "How? The board will never approve it!"

"I'm sure you'll find a way if you want to keep her."

"Of course we want to keep her!" He slaps his desk. "Yes, yes." He types something into the computer. He opens his drawer, takes out a notebook. "I'll talk to Coach. We'll figure it out. Might have to keep it hush-hush, if you get my meaning."

"Even better."

He snaps at his secretary. "Get Coach down here ASAP."

"Thanks, Cooper." He waves me out the door.

And just like that the white lie has been canceled. Everything is now perfect:

19

- Marta has her JOs—Check!
- I have my TV series—Double check!
- My white lie has been totally wiped clean and the day has only just begun—Triple check!

I run out to try and catch her. The upper yard is almost completely empty. "Marta!"

Marta comes huffing past me like an angry ox. She doesn't even stop when she sees me. "Marta!" I call after her. "Will you stop already? What's up with you?"

She suddenly spins around. "You want to know what's up with me?" She looks like she's gonna hit me. "The JOs are in two weeks. That's what's up with me."

The massive vein on Marta's forehead is popping out. "But Greta won't pay for it. She thinks we live in Romania, where everything is paid for. I'm like, 'Hello, we're in America! You have to pay for everything yourself here.' I want to kill her. I hate her."

"What if I were to tell you"—I pause and watch her face—"that there's a very good chance you're going?"

She drops her roller backpack on my foot. "If you don't shut your mouth—"

"Jeez, Marta!" Ouch. I lift my foot. "I'm not kidding. I just left Pickler's office. He wants you to be there."

She covers her mouth. She's turning red and waving her hands like they're on fire.

20

She still can't believe it. "But how? How?"

"Because you're the best gymnast on the team." I lean in. "And I might have told him Harvard wants you."

"You didn't!" She punches me.

"I did." I laugh. Man, it feels good to be on the right side of right.

"When will he tell us? When will I know?"

"In the next few days." I push her off. Jeez, she's out of control, she's so happy. "Just don't say anything, all right?"

"Of course I won't." Marta narrows her eyes and stands tall and proud. "You won't be sorry." She picks up her backpack and starts running.

"Wait," I yell out. "I almost forgot."

She comes running back like a puppy. "What, Charlie?"

I pause, take a breath, slow my heart—"Do you think you could teach me a routine on the beam?"

QUESTION: Do I feel guilty? Is that what you want to know? The answer is Yes and No. If it all goes according to plan, we're both winners.

She gets this weird look on her face. "A routine on the beam? You?"

"I know." I roll my eyes. "It's for a dumb thing Chad wants me to do."

"An audition?" She looks immediately suspicious. "He

didn't say anything to me. I thought he represented us both."

"He does. Of course. But this is to play a kid who wants to be a gymnast but is totally hopeless. You are a great gymnast."

"But . . ." Now she looks hurt. "I could play someone who isn't."

"You'd rather do this than go to the Olympics?" Her face changes before my eyes. "Because you have to go on hundreds of auditions, get head shots, work the whole acting thing, grovel, before you actually book something. You can die on an audition—you should see how many old people there are just nodding off into eternal sleep. But you, Marta"—I grab her shoulders for emphasis—"you're following in your mother's footsteps. You're going to the JOs."

She thinks about it and agrees. "You're absolutely right. I don't have time to waste on that nonsense. I don't know what got into me." She stomps up the stairs, stops on the first landing, and turns around. "I'm going to Texas!" she sings. "You know they're making me keep a three point seven-five average—otherwise I get booted from the team? And Greta is making me train for two hours every morning before school."

"See?" I chase after her, feeling way better already. "You wouldn't have the time to make some dumb commercial anyway. That's why they never asked you. You're going to be an Olympian one day."

She pulls open the door. The hallway is lined with weird

self-portraits by the fourth graders. "Course I'll help you, Charlie."

"You have enough time?"

"After what you did for me—"

Down the hall behind us, our classroom door opens. Mr. Lawson comes out. "Ms. Cooper? Ms. Urloff?" His angry voice bounces off the cold hallway. "Are you two planning on gracing us with your star power anytime soon?"

"We were in Pickler's office," I yell back, "and not for anything bad, I swear."

"Now that would be a first." He taps his shoe. "I'm waiting."

"Coming, Mr. L." Marta walks faster.

"Wait." I pull her pink sweater. "How long do you think it will take to make me look believable?"

"As a gymnast?" She snorts. "Years. Decades." She has a blueberry stuck to her back molar. "Your DNA is all wrong."

"First of all, offensive," I point out. "And secondly, you know me. I am a very fast learner."

"Ms. Cooper?" Mr. L is growing impatient. "American history is full of people almost as great as yourself."

"Don't worry." Marta nods confidently. "I'll make it so they'll never know you're not a real gymnast."

Mr. L is losing his Buddhist calm. "*Now*, or it's detention."

Detention? Seriously? Does he not know who he's talking to?

"Remember," I call out quietly, "hush-hush."

Marta runs.

"Charlie!" He points right at me. "Now!"

"Consider me there."

But first I must reapply my new MAC matte red Rock and Roll lip crayon that is awesome.

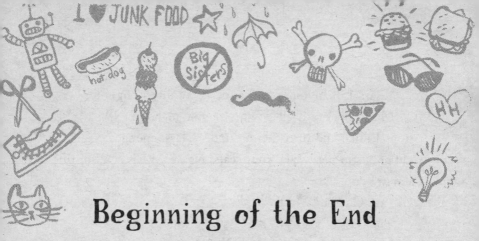

Beginning of the End

I saunter into class, all cool and calm. Do I expect a standing ovation for my heroics in the tunnels? No. I'm so not that egotistical. But a huge round of applause, a few mentions of how great I looked on CNN? Maybe a cupcake tray?

What I do not expect is that Marta's big fat mouth is already flapping big-time.

Lillian, the team captain, is screaming. "You are not coming to the JOs. No way. Coach said so, and it's final."

"I wouldn't be so sure." Marta pushes back.

Erica, Lillian's second-in-command, yells in her face, "You can't afford it."

"I wouldn't be so sure," she says again like she has some inside knowledge.

"Liar." Lillian hops over her desk, coming straight for her. Marta doesn't back down. It's not in her DNA. Mr. L stops Lillian and turns her around. "Class, enough, enough!" He points to me. "Take your seats, please. What is all of this about?"

"Ask Charlie," Marta says.

The class is quiet. "What? Ask me what?"

Lillian's face is so tight it looks like a mask. "Is she or is she not coming to the JOs in two weeks?"

I shrug. "I have no idea what you're talking about."

Lillian looks like she wants to erase me from sight. "So"—I smile like a superstar—"who watched the news over the week-end?"

"Five minutes of fame, babe." Lillian looks at my feet. "Big Deal. And Marta's NOT coming."

"Not bad, Cooper." Bobby taps his pencil on his desk. "You even looked like a girl. Had a waist and everything."

He's fallin' for me. I kid you not. And I'm gonna kiss him if it's the last thing I do.

Bobby starts drawing a skull. He's wearing this leather necklace with a shark's tooth on it. So hot. "Just be careful out there in Hollywood land— "

"Ssh," I whisper. Last thing I need is Lillian, Erica, or Babette knowing my business.

He shakes his head. "They suck you dry and leave you dead inside."

26

"Bobby. Ssh."

"Class, speak quietly amongst yourselves while I finish writing this amazing poem by Mr. Ralph Waldo Emerson on the board." L's back is turned. Talk about out of touch. Waldo? And who the heck reads cursive? Html, baby, that's where it's at.

"Just watch out." Bobby shades in the skull, darkens the teeth of his death pic.

"Well, Mr. Depressing." I lean back and fix my black sequin butterfly barrette. "Good news. I don't have to. I have a great agent who watches my back. He'd never let anything happen to me. Ever."

"Yeah, right." Bobby pulls up his hood and keeps on drawing the corn teeth.

The bell rings, Lillian mumbles something to Erica, and they take off like there's a fire. Something's going on. I look for Marta and see her running out the door.

"Marta, hold up!"

"Hey, Coop." Bobby, beautiful Bobby gets in my way, and I forget all about Marta.

Bobby Digs Me Big-Time

The hallway empties about as fast as it fills.

"What's up with you?"

"Nothing." He gets all jumpy. "Nothing's up. "

"You know you can tell me, right?" I pretend to read one of the fourth graders' super dull personal narratives hanging in the hallway. The title of this one: "How Video Games Are Evil." Yeah, right.

"Kids spouting their parents' lies." Bobby smiles.

I turn my back on the wall of narratives. "I'll never tell your secret. Cross my heart." I cross it, making sure I don't bring attention to the bumps.

But he's looking at me. And let me tell you, he's got this look on his face that's making my mouth dry up faster than a desert pond. It's like he's going to kiss me. I wonder if my breath stinks. Oh, God. My breath stinks. I take a step back.

"Dude"—he kicks the wall with his high-tops—"why do you want to go and do something dumb like Hollywood?" He wipes his eyes with both fingers like guys always do. "It's full of scumbags."

"Oh, come on, Bobby! I might have my own trailer!" I jump up and down like a fool. "And a golf cart! You know how they all cruise around in golf carts? What part of that doesn't sound awesome?"

He shrugs and says, "I thought you were different."
Ouch.

"They messed up my dad. All his old friends hate him now. Stay true, Cooper."

"True's my middle name." I pick up my pack. The hallway is empty now, and my stomach is mad that I'm not feeding it.

Bobby and I walk toward the exit. He's about a foot taller than me—man, do I like tall men. He starts bouncing the ball that lives under his armpit. "Wanna maybe shoot some hoops after school?"

Do I want to maybe shoot some hoops? Do I breathe? Of course I want to shoot some hoops— "Oh, shoot! I almost forgot. I have to go to Marta's house." I look into his huge brown eyes.

Suddenly his whole attitude changes. "No, that's cool. She needs all the help she can get. See ya around." He takes his basketball and bounces it out the door.

I take a seat next to Marta at our always-empty lunch spot. She sneezes into her long-sleeved shirt, then rolls up the sleeve where the snot shot out. "What took you so long?"

I take out my foot-long mozzarella sandwich on La Brea sourdough. "You know you really should keep your big mouth shut."

"Why?"

We watch Lillian and her crew huddled together across the way. "Because they're up to something, dumb butt, that's why, and the less they know about you and me, the better."

TRUE FACT: Let's get this straight—Lillian's no Trixie. She doesn't care about things like popularity. She only cares about being the best on the team. And thanks to Marta, she's not anymore.

Marta wolfs down her tuna sandwich like a great white. "Who the heck cares?" She smacks away, her mouth a tunnel of mayo and fish.

I can't believe she's so dense. "They want you gone, Marta. They've always wanted you gone."

"The way I see it, it's a game." Marta crunches a carrot in my ear. "A game of how long the other guy can last." She swallows, knocks back some warm milk. "They want to get rid of me, and I want to move so far ahead of them that it'll just be me and Coach. It's what I call a zero-sum game."

Zero-sum game. To me it looks like *all* of them against *her*.

"But at the end of the day . . ." She shoves the crust down her throat with her finger. "I'm the best. They know it. Coach knows it. Nothing can stop me."

TRUE FACT: Saying "nothing can stop me" is like begging for something to stop you. I should know— I'm a middle child.

I get up and toss my trash. "Believe what you want, but don't"—I come back and punch her on the shoulder to drive this point across—"and I mean *don't* mention the JOs until you have the ticket in your hand and the entrance fee receipt paid. Don't tell them a thing, Marta, or they'll find a way to stop you. Keep that big mouth shut." I grab her chin. "You got me?"

"Yeah, yeah." She says it like I'm nuts.

I drain the last of my Pellegrino and watch Bobby dip and dodge. The way he wears the loose basketball shorts with the totally dinged-up Converse makes me crazy.

Marta rips off a chunk of apple. She zeroes in on Lillian and her crew, pointing her finger right at them. "Who's the new girl?"

I whack her finger. "Her name's Lola, she's supposed to be in eighth grade, but she got held back." She's got bigger boobs than my mom, which makes her the most popular kid in school.

31

Marta nods. "She's totally staring at Bobby."

They all are. Every time he gets near the hoops, they jump up and clap like he's just found a cure for cancer.

The first bell rings. Marta takes off. She's a stickler for bells.

I shove the last bite of my sandwich into my mouth. It's truly important that each bite has a piece of mozzarella, a piece of tomato, and a piece of basil—otherwise it's sadness.

The bell rings: we all scatter like roaches.

The Birth of an Olympian

I have three days to do what Gabby Douglas took a lifetime to accomplish. And I'm not exaggerating. On day one, I arrive at Marta's brown door and bang on it. "Marta!" I can hear her feet pounding even before I see her. She yanks open the door.

"You're late." She's already in her gym clothes. Marta points down the darkened hallway. Her aunt hasn't made it that homey. In fact, it looked cleaner when Marta lived here alone. There are candy wrappers everywhere, empty Coke cans, bags of chips and trashy Hollywood magazines. And then I see the photo — a very small woman with Marta's eyes and dead gray complexion standing on a podium, in a red-and-white leotard, with a silver medal around her neck. Her mom, at the Olympics. What a lady.

I wipe the dust off the frame with the bottom of my T-shirt. Marta's glaring at me. "What are you doing?"

I forgot how protective she is about her pictures, so I put it back exactly where I found it. "So where's your aunt?"

"Getting a mani-pedi." Marta throws back the sliding door. "It's like her second one since she got here. *And* they cost a fortune. *And* she has no money. It's always me, me, me." She stops, scratches her head.

Even I can tell she's stressed. "Yo, isn't she here to take care of you?"

Marta snaps her fingers. "I've thought it over, and I think the beam's your best bet."

"I hate the beam."

"You need to know how to get on it, how to get off it, and how to look like you know what you're doing in between."

What a major drag. The whole point of being a star is *not* having to do anything. I pick up the giant brown receiver from the Dark Ages and stick my fingers in the holes and call my mom. I tell her I'll be home in time for dinner.

Marta grabs the phone out of my hand. "More like bedtime, Mrs. Cooper!" She cracks her neck. "Now, get out to the gym. Meet the beam."

Meet the beam? She's so weird. I go out—the beam's there dividing up her small yard. "Hey, Beam." I look under it, around it. I strip off my outerwear to expose my faux black snakeskin leotard with the slogan Gymnastics Rox in diamonds.

34

"What the hell is that?" Marta says when she sees it.

"Don't be so jealous." I massage my diamonds. "I'll get you one."

"Over my dead body." She points to the beam. "Get on."

"Sure." I like how the leotard holds my belly in. "Where's the stool?"

"Stool?" Marta rolls her eyes. "There is no stool."

Great.

"Today you're going to learn how to mount the beam without looking like a giant sausage. Tomorrow, how to leap without looking like a giant sausage, and then how to dismount—"

I got it. "Without looking like a giant sausage."

TRUE FACT: The abused can become pretty nasty abusers when given half the chance. Keep reading.

Marta yanks my arms across the beam. "Now lift yourself up and straddle the beam."

I stare at it. "Say what?"

"Like this." She stands in front of it, pushes herself up, and lifts her right leg up and over until she's straddling it. "This is the easiest way on."

Liar. "What about the little springy thing?"

She ignores me and hops down. "Now you."

I put my hands on the beam, and I heave myself up, turn slightly, and straddle. "See?"

"You look like a dying whale."

"Experts agree." I pull myself up, square my shoulders. "Sarcasm is not a great motivator."

"Now down." She circles me like a predator. "And back up.

"And down.

"And back up.

"I want to see you lift off the ground. I want to see your hip swivel out and your leg straddle in one motion."

Somewhere along the way Marta's found a stick. She's tapping the floor in a pretty scary way.

"Leg over, straddle." She watches me like a vulture. The sun is gone. I've got a major rash. "Tomorrow we work on moving from straddle position to leg up, walk beam, leap, dismount."

Free at last. I hop off, sore as heck.

She whacks the backs of my legs with her stick. "Get back on! On and off until you don't look like you're dying."

"FYI," I point out immediately, "you're becoming super mean." By the end of the night, I want to quit. Give up. I'm not cut out for hard work. But this is what keeps me going, people:

TELEVISION. It's the only cure for the torture of life.

"Take a hot bath and we'll pick up where we left off tomorrow morning at five."

"Five? As in three whole hours before the bell rings?"

"Go." She picks me up and opens the door to a pitch-black

driveway. I was kinda hoping her aunt would be home from the salon with a hot pizza and a ride home. But she never shows. "So how do I get home?"

"It's called the bus." She pauses to let the horror of it sink in and simmer. "And you need the thirty-nine. Comes every half an hour on the other side of the street. If you leave now, you might make it. And I'd try to make it. It gets cold out there on the street." The door closes without the slightest bit of hesitation. Man, she's cold.

"Wow, thanks." I walk out onto the mean streets of Reseda.

By the time I get home and kiss Mom and Dad good night, I'm so tired I can barely stand. But it's a good tired. I walk into the bathroom, run a warm bath, and slip into it. Every muscle aches, but it's a good ache. I close my eyes and dream.

Day Two of My Rebirth

Yes, people, for the next two days I'm up before even the sun. I go downstairs, open the fridge, and eat. Then I take the 4:30 bus to Marta's house in Reseda to train.

Marta's aunt sure doesn't mess around. Every morning, she's fully dressed in a gym outfit with the word ROMANIA written in red. She always offers me tea.

On day two, Marta drops to the mat and starts her push-ups. Her stomach doesn't even sag onto the mat.

Marta raises the stick and points it at my core—yes, my core—and has the indecency to announce, "If you want to work the beam, you're gonna have to lose some of that fat."

Offensive, or what? "First of all," I point out, "my doctor says I'm not fat. Plus, I told you. They like my belly. I'm the

38

evil, jealous sister, remember?"

"Come on, you weakling, sit-ups. Fifty." And she launches right into it, as effortlessly as me opening a bag of Doritos. I start, but at ten I swear it feels like my stomach is being ripped apart. I collapse on the mat until she gets to forty-five, then I start back up again, huffing and puffing, like I never quit. "Now that was tough," I announce like a true athlete.

Marta finishes her set, lies on her back, stretching. She looks up at the sky and says with the calmest voice, "Do you want this?" She turns to look at me. "Because if you do, you're going to have to fight for it," Marta says. "Blood, sweat, and tears."

She's right. Blood, sweat, and tears. I get up and walk to the beam. I want this. I want this more than I have ever wanted anything in my life. I mount the beam.

Marta hits the stick against the mat, and I do it again and again for hours.

By the time it's 7:45, I'm about ready to puke. To rethink my goal. To just call in sick for the rest of my life. It's so hot, and my legs can barely hold me up. My arms don't feel attached to my body. "We'll continue after school." Marta puts down her whip. "Greta will drive."

Greta's dangling the keys over the door. "I am excellent driver."

Graffiti Alley

I can't count how many times we almost crashed. From now on, I will never, and I mean ever, complain about the bus again. In fact, I love my bus driver with his narrow eyes and his rearview suspicion.

By lunch, my legs feel like they've got weights attached to them. I can barely make it down the stairs. Kids run past me, bumping and knocking me off guard. In the middle of it I see Mr. Bobby Brown. He's smiling right at me. "Hey, old lady, you want to come someplace with me?"

It's a miracle! My legs are fine! I need a kiss. I want a kiss.

He takes my hand. We run down the corridor. I forget all about my aching muscles and follow Bobby's lead. We run past

Pickler's office and go up one flight of stairs. He looks over the railing. "Ready?"

"Where?" All I can see is the mountain and a lot of dirt.

He climbs over the railing and throws himself off.

"What the—" I look over the ledge. And there he is, hot as ever, standing against a rock wall.

Bobby puts his finger up to his lips. "Get down here before we get busted."

I look both ways, about to climb the railing, when Mr. L comes walking down the stairs and stops right in front of me. I freeze.

He looks over at the railing, putting two and two together. "You're not jumping into Graffiti Alley, are you?"

"Me? No way, sir." I point to the door. "I'm heading to the library." I wait till he's gone.

"Cooper!" Bobby calls me.

I run to the railing, check quickly, and this time I do it. I jump straight into Graffiti Alley. All I can think of as I fly through the sky is, Thank the lord I'm wearing my RCVA overalls I had hemmed and wear like a glove. Zero possibility of an underwear flash.

Bobby's all business. He grabs my hand the second I land and we disappear down a long, narrow passage until we're hidden between the back of the middle school and the mountain. Bobby sits, his back against the dirt wall. "No one can see us here."

I'm suddenly nervous. I did not, and I repeat did not, bring my brand-new MAC Rock and Roll lip crayon. Was this going to be it? The big moment? And I, Charlie C. Cooper, am lipstickless?

Bobby puts his hands over his knees, drops his head. "Ever heard of this place?"

The walls are covered in old-school Latino block graffiti and a funky take on the Mercedes-Benz symbol. There's trash everywhere, which leads me to believe there could be a super scary ax murderer living behind our school.

"Legend is there was a kid here at Happy Canyon who went totally nuts, ran away, and eventually ended up right here. Living in a tent. Free."

Free in a tent?

He reaches into his backpack and takes out a can of black paint and starts spray-painting over the Mercedes-Benz symbols, covering them in black paint.

"What are you doing?" I try to stop him. "Do you even know how much trouble we're gonna get in?"

But Bobby doesn't care. He keeps on spraying until the can is empty and the symbols are gone. "It's my dad's trademark."

"Wait a sec, why are you blacking them out, then?" Looks like the Mercedes-Benz logo to me.

"Because I hate every last one of 'em." He puts the empty

can in his backpack and checks his fingers. The bell rings.

I look up. You can hear the storm of feet coming up from the lower yard. The screams as they approach the stairwell, all trying to get to class on time.

Bobby grabs me and we hide under the stairs. He holds me close. I swear to God, he's gonna kiss me. This is where I, Charlie C. Cooper, am getting my first kiss.

But then the final bell rings. The stomping stops, and Bobby lets me go. "Now!" He climbs up and checks both ends of the stairs. As soon as I am up, he takes off.

No kiss. Dang it.

After school, Greta picks us up at 2:40 in Marta's mom's old orange corn-drinking Pacer car from the Dark Ages. It's almost more humiliation than I can bear. Lucky for me, we slip out before anyone can see us. I duck as low as I can in the backseat. She revs the engine, and suddenly we're flying off the curb and crashing down on the street.

I turn and see a piece of the car in the middle of the road.

I elbow Marta. "Does your aunt even have insurance?"

"You wanna take the bus?" Marta glares at me.

I close my eyes and think, Yeah, I kinda do.

Greta sees my face. "In Romania I have all insurance. State pays for it. Not like here, where you have to pay for everything. Here is not free. There is free." I look up as Greta taps one four-inch red nail against the wheel.

"Only thing here better is manicure salon. In Romania, very, very expensive."

Marta hits me. "Did you and Bobby go somewhere today?"

I don't even open my eyes. "No."

"Boys and training do not mix." Greta frowns suspiciously.

Marta turns and whispers, "Lillian told me his dad takes drugs."

My eyes fly open, and I sit up as straight as a rod. "What did you just say?"

"She said his father takes drugs." Greta adjusts the mirror so she can see my face. "No big deal. In Romania, many people take drugs."

"What?" I grab her shirt and pull her toward me. "When did you hear this?"

"Today, when everyone was going on about how the two of you went missing. Missing and kissing—"

I'm about to hit her when Greta cuts in *again*.

"Don't get mixed up in that nonsense, Charlie. Drugs are for losers."

Like I don't know that. "And everyone knows?"

Marta nods.

Poor Bobby. Poor, poor Bobby.

"That is what you do here in America. You raise them up

and you tear them down." Greta tickles her mole with her giant red blade.

I slide back down. It all makes sense now.

We pull into the driveway. Greta opens the door and announces, "After-school snack time. Sit in front of TV. I will bring it."

We walk through the deep chocolate-brown carpet and collapse onto the sofa. Marta picks up a remote and clicks on the TV. "You ever see this show?"

I stare at the screen. It's *Make It or Break It*. I can't believe she even knows the show exists.

She grins like a psycho. "I could watch it all day. It feels like my life. The mean girls and me."

"But they're actresses, Marta. You're the real thing." I'm feeling a little hot flash coming on.

"Ssh!" She throws her hand up to cut me off. "This is a really good part."

Marta's aunt calls from the kitchen. "Protein, girls."

Marta pauses the show.

"Tuna and mayo on white," Greta announces proudly as she walks into the room carrying the platter of food. "Glasses of warm milk. Very American, no, Charlie?"

I take the plate and close off all air coming into my nostrils. There are simply no words to express my disdain for tuna.

"Eat." Greta stares. "Eat."

I plug my nose and close my eyes. I lift the sandwich to my lips.

Marta jabs me. "You have to eat tuna if you want to be a great gymnast."

I want to run away. But instead, I do what she tells me and give in. I take a bite of tuna and wash it down with warm milk.

This, my friends, is called growth.

Six hours later, I limp home. I can't wait to walk in my front door and crawl up to bed. I have never been so tired in my whole life. "Hey, Mom," I say weakly, and hobble past her, my eyes on the stairs, willing my legs to make it up.

She stops me. "What's wrong with your ankles?"

I stop and lift one up. Blood has come through both socks. "Marta likes to whack my heels. It's like some kinda cruel training tip her aunt picked up from the Russians back in the day."

"Oh, baby," she cries, "I am so sorry." She dabs on Neosporin and covers them with Band-Aids. They feel cured already.

"Are you hungry? Of course you're hungry! Sit, let me feed you." She goes to the fridge and pulls out the most beautiful lasagna made in the shape of a coffin. "I'm practicing for the Halloween party. What do you think?"

Man, I love my mom sometimes. Not all the time, of course, but sometimes a lot. Especially times like these, when

I'm hungry, tired, and she's got a whole lasagna and a fork waiting for me.

Later that night, when Pen's snoring and Felix has stopped playing pretend video games under his covers, I tiptoe out of my bed, grab my laptop. The magic of Google lights up before my eyes. I take a deep breath, not so sure I really want to know. But I do, I *do* want to know. I type in "Brown" (I don't know his first name) "Laurel Canyon Graffiti Artist." Then I type in "drugs."

The screen lights up like a Christmas tree. Bobby's dad's name is Mercy, Merc for short. And then I remember the symbols Bobby was spraying over. They didn't stand for *Mercedes-Benz*—they stood for *Merc Brown*. They were his symbols. He studied art at Yale. Was a painter. Moved out to LA to study street art in East LA. "His star was on the rise," the article from the *Times* says, "and when he met famed music producer, blah, blah, blah, he became the number-one graphic artist in the industry, until he was recently fired."

Why? I scroll down. "Why was he fired?" I click on the second article. I go to the bottom until I see the word *drugs*. I slap my computer shut. Marta is right. It is none of my business.

And yet.

I close my eyes but can't sleep.

And yet, it is my business. We're friends.

I pick my computer back up and write:

Bobby,
Now I get it. I'm here if you want.

I hit send and feel a whole lot better.

Own That Beam

Day three.

It's dark again when I wake up for my last training session. I grab my flashlight and search for something to wear. Penelope finds me downstairs, watering the plants. I hear my toast pop up. "You want some toast?"

"Yeah, thanks." She pulls out a chair, turns on her computer. Pen's computer is actually newer than mine, which is so unbelievable I can barely mention it without feeling sick. "I've got to get this proposal finished by today."

I line up four pieces of warm bread and slather on butter and watch it melt. Then I slather on Nutella and watch it cling to the butter like best friends. I take a bite of one just to see.

Yep, it's a trip straight to heaven. I hand her a plate. "So what's the proposal about?"

"We have to get the city to stop handing out building permits in the canyons that are allowing them to kill our wildlife." She nibbles. "Thanks."

I inhale the next piece. "By wildlife you mean rats?"

She rolls her eyes and says, "You're heartless."

I take my plate to the sink. "Nah, I'm just kidding, Pen." And that's the truth. If Pen didn't take up these dead-end causes, she'd be in my business 24/7, so I was one hundred percent behind it.

Half an hour later, Marta's already abusing me. In fact, Marta has become so comfortable being the dominant one in our relationship that she screams from the top of her pink lungs and whacks me with a stick every time I see her. Her aunt sits in a recliner, feet up, *People* magazine in her lap, watching us like it's totally okay that I'm being beaten to death. "Your cartwheel is sloppy. Your legs need to be straight, Charlie. How many times have I told you?" She pushes me. I slip on my own sweat and fall flat on my butt, *slap!* Marta tosses her stick down in disgust, goes inside, and pulls the door shut.

Then I look up and see Marta's aunt standing over me. All I can think of is her mole and how it's going to roll off her cheek and drop onto my face. "Gymnastics is not possible for you. You look like giant bag of soft Russian potatoes."

She sees my crushed face. "You Americans think you can have talent if you wish on star. But you cannot." She stirs her iced tea with her long, fake red fingernail. "We Romanians know working hard is the only way out. Give audition to Marta. She can make money for JOs and pay for manicure-pedicure."

She's right. I should give it to Marta. She would kill the audition. She needs the money.

Marta comes out. She sees the look on my face. "Again."

I look into her eyes. "Marta, there's something I want to ask you—"

"Not now." She points her stick. "Practice leaps and dismount. You have to forget you're off the ground, that's all."

I sit down, and I ask, "Do you want the audition? Because you can have it if you want it."

Marta looks at me. She folds her arms over her chest. "I want the Olympics. That's all I want. So please can we get on with this?"

I smile. "So you're not jealous about the audition?"

"Me?" She pushes me to the beam. "No way. Now mount."

A thousand pounds lifted just like that.

"Beam." She points, and I go.

I get up and over the beam without leaning on my chest.

"Good." She hits the stick.

I go into a straddle, lift one leg up, get up and try like heck to balance my shaking legs. I plant my hands and manage a pretty good cartwheel. I do another, gaining confidence, and then another. I can't believe I haven't fallen. I do a little bouncing thing I copied from Nadia Comăneci and then I ready myself for the dismount.

"Now cartwheel into roundoff," she says. I judge my footing, and I plant my hands, do the cartwheel off the end, and land on both feet. I raise my hands like an Olympian. I watch her face. There is no expression. So I think:

- It was horrible.
- I'll never make it.
- I want a jumbo bag of Doritos.

And then she claps, softly at first, and then hard like a grown man. Like Coach. "Brava! You did it."

Yes! I hug her, fall back on the mat, and look up at the morning sky. "I did it." One down. Two to go. And so far, Lillian and her crew have no idea at all. I'm practically home free.

I get up. My legs feel like jelly. I'm in so much pain, I don't even notice that Greta's been filming us all along.

One Down. One to Go.

As soon as the bell rings, I gear up to tackle the next major hurdle on my road to Hollywood. Paying for the head shots. I lunge for the door and run through the hallway before it gets mobbed with directionless tweens.

"Charlie!" Marta calls after me.

I ignore her. All I want to do is make it out of the upper yard and into my mom's car.

But then, out of the blue, I hear Bobby's voice. "Yo, Cooper, where you always running to so fast?"

There he is, carrying a basketball. "Where the heck have you been?" Those butterflies are instantly coursing through me. I'd waited for him at both Nutrition and lunch, but he

53

wasn't there. In fact, he wasn't anywhere. I even checked Graffiti Alley.

"Just had to disappear for a little while. My parents. It's a mess," he says like he's struggling. I know that feeling. "You wanna take a walk?"

"Oh, man, Bobby, I'm so sorry," I say, and I mean it. "But I can't. My mom's waiting for me."

"Where are you going?" he says slowly, like he's got nothing to do. Meanwhile I have millions of things to do. Fame isn't just handed to you, you know? Hollywood doesn't just open its doors. You have to break them down.

"Career stuff." I try to move forward, but Bobby takes my backpack hostage.

I feel bad, I do. Believe me, if it weren't MY DESTINY, I would hang with him for eternity. "Another time, all right?"

He takes the ball and slaps it against the wall. "Maybe I'll ask Lola."

I can feel the burn. But I pretend he didn't say it and keep on walking.

Mr. L hears the smack of the ball. "The paint is white, Mr. Brown," Mr. L says quietly. "No balls allowed."

"Yeah, yeah." Bobby just keeps bouncing the ball all the way down the hallway.

I take a deep breath and push my way to the door, which is now jammed with people who have no destiny at all. I slap

54

myself. That was mean. But at least I didn't say it out loud, right?

I scan the parking lot for my mom and find her in her car, dangling half on and half off the curb. Major no-no here at Happy Canyon. Mom sees me and honks twice. I'm about to run to her when, behind me, I hear Pen's voice. I turn and see Felix running after her. I stare in disbelief. "I thought we were going alone?" I yell to no one, because clearly *no one* ever listens to me. This was supposed to be something I was going to do alone. With Mom.

Mom honks. She's waving at us like a crazy woman. "Come on, I'm double-parked here! Bad karma, people."

And then, to add insult to injury, Pen goes and jumps in the front seat. "What the heck?" I stand in the hot parking lot and yell at the top of my lungs, "Get out!"

"Come on, Charlie, don't be a pill." Mom shakes her head like it's me being unreasonable when this is what Pen does all the time and then I get blamed for it.

"Are you serious?" I look at her. "What happened to this being just you and me?"

Mom rolls her eyes. "Just get in!" Someone honks. Mom starts to sweat. "In now, or we're going straight home."

"This is so not fair!" I yank the back door open as hard as I can. I want the handle to fall off. I throw my bag against the seat. "I got stuff to do, Pen. Like get a job."

Pen throws her hands up. "Technically it's not a job."

I want to strangle her. "If you make a scene—" Pen always made scenes at the Pumpkin Patch. Every year, from Malibu all the way to West LA. Nothing like an overpriced pumpkin mixed with underage labor to set her off.

"No scene," Pen promises.

I pull myself up and squeeze into the empty space between Mom and Pen. "Mom," I whisper sweetly.

"Yeees—" She knows what's coming.

"In case they're not hiring any more free child labor or if I don't make enough in tips, you'll loan me the rest? Right?" I beg like a pup. "I swear I'll pay you back."

Mom doesn't look convinced. "I think it's important for you to follow this through."

"But Mom . . ." I pull myself way forward. "It's basically a done deal. I'm going to make a fortune."

"Live in the present," she says quietly.

I hate that expression so much that it stops me from begging. I just slump back and stare out the window. That homeless guy is still on the corner of Sunset Boulevard. Today, he's wearing old cowboy boots and brown cords and is playing a game with his one-eyed dog.

Pen lowers the mirror and checks out her mustache that grows faster than the lawn. "How much are the pictures?"

"A couple hundred bucks," I lie. "But in less than a year, I could be in a limo wearing a phenomenal dress on my way to the Emmys."

"I can give you my money, Charlie." Felix pokes me with his pencil.

I'm momentarily speechless. Then I lean in so close I can smell his hair. "When I'm rich and famous," I whisper, "I'm gonna remember you most of all."

Mom's still staring me down. "One way or the other, you're going to have to earn it."

Just the sound of that word *earn* gives me the shakes. It has such a horrible ring to it. *Earn.*

Mom slows at a stop sign. A homeless woman is babbling to herself. Mom looks at us in the rearview mirror. "Does anyone have any food left in their lunch box?"

Pen starts dipping into hers, Felix into his.

"Oh, God, please don't." I fall back in my seat.

"Kindness, Charlie." She gets out. We watch her talk to the woman and hand her the bag of food. The woman takes it, opens it like she's inspecting it carefully. And then, suddenly, she throws it right back in Mom's face.

Pen is horrified. Felix doesn't understand it. And me, well, all I see is Mom's face. She's stunned. And worse, she's shaking. She walks back, gets in the car, and drives without explanation.

About half a block later, I can't stand the silence anymore.

I tap her shoulder. There's food on it. I brush it off. "Why did she do that to you?"

"She said"—Mom pulls into the Pumpkin Patch lot—"I was disrespecting her with leftovers, which is fine."

I throw my arms around her neck and hug her tightly.

She pats my hands. "I'm okay, Charlie, I'm okay. Come, let's go."

I don't believe her. "You sure?"

"Your father and I backpacked through all of India and Tibet. I've had my fair share of food thrown in my face."

I check her face and hair. "You should call the police."

Mom hugs me. "It's okay—go on ahead. I'll meet you over there."

"Yeah, go knock 'em dead, Charlie." Pen smiles.

TRUE FACT: She's enjoying this a little too much.

I take a deep breath and get out of the car. I'm a little nervous, I must confess. I've never had an actual job before. And it's so dang hot the straw looks like it's about to catch fire. Babies are screaming their high-pitched wails, kids are sweating through their Halloween costumes, and parents are melting behind their cameras. It's like hell with pumpkins.

"Global warming sure has taken the fun out of Halloween." Pen shields her eyes. "It's so depressing coming to the Patch just to see all these pumpkins rotting out here in the sun." She spots something on a pumpkin. "Look, maggots. Flies are leaving their eggs everywhere!"

Parents all around us scoop up their kids and run to the anti-bacterial stations. I elbow her hard. "You promised, remember?"

And then, as if God is not punishing me enough, I hear Lillian's voice ringing through the heat waves. "Charlie Cooper? Is that you?" She's flanked by her car and driver. Everyone knows her parents are a sickening team of Hollywood power, and when I say sickening, I mean fantastic. There's no escaping it. Lillian comes bouncing over in an all-white sundress. She looks like a commercial.

"Hey, Charlie, Penelope, what are you guys doing here?" she says, all cool, like there's no water under the bridge at all. But there is. There's so much water I can barely look at her without feeling like I'm drowning.

"Charlie's trying to get a job here." Pen taps one of the pumpkins with the top of her toe. It rolls over. There's a little tag that says forty dollars.

"Forty bucks!" Pen cringes.

"A job?" She's immediately hooked. "Here?"

I want to kill her. I want to run over and stab her.

"Now why would Charlie need a job?" She's pondering the question like it's delicious.

"For head shots, of course." Pen just keeps on digging the hole that's going to bury me. "Now that she's famous, they want her to do a TV show about gymnastics."

No one would blame me for killing her right now.

Lillian looks curious. "My agent didn't mention anything to me."

TRUE FACT: Everyone's got an agent in LA.

"They want her to be the evil dorky sister who tries to sabotage all the girls because they won't give her a shot."

Lillian looks relieved. "Yeah, I so don't do evil dorky. But for you, Charlie, it's perfect."

I want to sew her lips shut.

Lillian stops and cocks her head. "Weird they didn't ask Marta. Do they know you can't even do a cartwheel?"

Offensive. "I can so do a cartwheel. And they want someone *not* good—you get it?" I say angrily.

"I don't know." She kicks the dirt. "It's so much easier to pretend you're not good than pretend you're good. And you, Charlie"—she taps me on the shoulder with each word—"don't know the first thing about gymnastics." Lillian narrows her eyes and watches the panic set into my face, sees me tighten my jaw. She's tasted blood. She knows. "You have to tell her, Charlie."

"Why?" Sweat drips down my face like tears. "Marta's not

60

interested. She's training for the—"

"I told you," she says with a deadly calm. "She's not going to the JOs." Lillian smiles with team captain certainty. "She'll have lots of free time."

"But"—I, too, plaster on a fake smile—"Coach really wants her to go."

Lillian suddenly stabs her high heel right through a baby pumpkin. It goes all the way through.

Pen can't take her eyes off the baby pumpkin stuck to Lillian's shoe. "You just murdered a baby pumpkin. How could you do that—"

I cut Pen off. "Mom's calling you."

"All right, I'm going." Pen backs away, her eyes on Lillian. "Hey, can we count on your support? For the wildlife corridor?"

She gives her two-thumbs-up. "Absolutely." Pen runs off. Lillian takes the pumpkin off her shoe and holds it in her hands like a crystal ball. "I see a rosy future for us both."

"Oh really?"

"You, with your own TV series, and me, as Coach's pick for the JOs. And all either of us has to do is say nothing. Nothing."

I don't like the way she's looking at me. It's like she's trying to crawl into my head. I start walking away.

But Lillian grabs my arm. She spins me around. "Did you know that in about"—she looks at her watch—"two hours, everyone from school, including Bobby, will descend on this place and see you shoveling pumpkin guts?"

A threat.

She smiles. Those blue eyes crawling all over me. "This is our after-school Halloween hangout."

Mom yells, "Charlie!"

I turn. The place is filling up.

"But if you want, I can keep them away." She puts her finger to her lips. "Would you like that, Charlie?"

Here it comes.

"In exchange for what?"

"Keep Marta out of the JOs." She shrugs. "And that's so easy. She can't afford it. You do absolutely nothing to help her." She grins like it's a beautiful thing. "You do *nothing*." The good news is she doesn't know that Pickler's already offered to pay. I'm one big step ahead of her. I keep playing.

"Or else?"

"Or else I tell Marta about your little acting gig. I encourage her to try out. And she'll get it," Lillian says matter-of-factly. "We both know she will. That's why you didn't tell her, isn't it?"

Yep, in a nutshell.

The sun is beating down on my shoulders. And although kids around me are crying, adults are laughing, and my mother is calling, all I can do is look at her face and consider the ultimatum she has given me:

Do nothing to help Marta go to the JOs. And for that she

will keep my lie a secret. And keep everyone I know away from the Pumpkin Patch.

A smile escapes me.

"So we have a deal?" Lillian reaches into her purse and takes out a pair of sunglasses that are so big, they cover half her face.

"We do."

"Perfect." She claps. "That's all I wanted to know." Then she changes gears completely. "Hey, you guys still throwing your Halloween party at the end of the week?"

The nerve of her. "Yep." I wave to Mom.

Lillian gives me that look I know so well. "You know we had nothing to do with all that Trixie craziness, right?"

"Of course," I say quickly, even though it's not true. Gnats are now sticking to my underarms like they're sucking the sweat from my shirt. I'm getting red spots all over my arms.

"I hope we're invited." Lillian watches me swat at them while they circle my pits like I've got gnat food hidden in there. She glances at her arms, her legs, and says, "I guess gnats don't like me."

I hate her even more. "Of course you're invited." I slap on the fake smile. "It's going to be great, fantastic." Mom's standing in front of the table where the big boss lady is sitting, talking to the people inside the hut. She sees me. Locks on to me. Mouth opens.

"See ya." I back away from Lillian and her car. I totally

have her right where I want her.

Mom is frantically waving me over. I run. When I get there, she grabs my wrists. I'm caught. She introduces me to my new boss. "This is Maria and her family." Mom points to four small kids, totally mute, the very same ones who were just stacking pumpkins into Lillian's limo. "Richie, Marcos, Diego, and Manuel."

The thought of Bobby, Erica, and Babs coming to laugh is distracting me from my single focus. It all hinges on Marta. As long as she keeps her big mouth shut, it'll all be perfect.

"Just follow their lead and do a great job." Mom says it like she's leaving me at a friend's house for a fun-filled sleepover. "I'll pick you up at seven."

I stare at my watch. I gasp at the heavens. "Seven?" That's like in four hours. "I haven't even eaten since two, Mom."

"Just think," she says all happily, "you're one step closer to having those head shots." Pen and Felix run toward her. As they get in the car, I see Lillian's limo pull out in a cloud of dust. Mom turns on the engine, rolls down the window, and waves. "We love you." And then they drive off, toward home.

I stand up as straight as I can. Suck back those tears, game face on.

"Hola, Carlita." Maria's husband, José, wakes me from my self-pity. "Time to get those pumpkins out of the heat. Boss gonna kill us." He tosses me a hat and some gloves. I look like Jason in *Friday the 13th*.

All I can do to stop myself from crying is to think about the money I'm going to be making and the head shots I'm going to be taking, and to pray to the Almighty that Marta keeps her big mouth shut. Kinda ironic that my little lie hangs on her.

Will I Never Learn?

The next day Bobby doesn't come to school again. Which really blows, because I spent a good hour twisting my hair into tight twisties all over my head, messing them up, and then, for a final touch, I populated my hair with purple sequin barrettes. *And* I wore my best black tutu, my RADICAL FEMINIST tank top, and of course my fishnets and Docs.

But no Bobby. So at lunch I sneak up to the library, and, using Ms. Myrtle's LAUSD email IP, I send Bobby a message:

> You better have a good excuse for leaving me here all
> alone. If you get this, shoot me a note ASAP before I'm forced

to return to Mr. L's most amazingly boring lecture on why we are our own masters. Whatever that means.

As I type the words, it hits me that I miss him. As in, actually miss him, like a friend. And yeah, the butterflies miss him, too.

"The bell's going to ring. Wrap it up, Charlie." Ms. Myrtle taps her pencil.

"Okay." I stand, willing something to come in.

"I'm closing." She taps louder.

I pick up my things, about to turn my back, when I hear the beep.

Hey Coop,

Family meeting. Family falling apart. I don't want to grow up. My parents are a mess. See you tomorrow.

P.S. Lola doesn't come close.

"Yes!" The final bell rings.

Ms. Myrtle's standing in the door. "Now, Charlie."

"Absolutely." I delete the email, erase all traces, and go happily back to class, but just as I open the classroom door, Lillian pulls me aside. "I held up my part of the deal. It'll be a ghost town there."

"Really?" I ask. People are looking at me. Marta's looking at me.

"Now you hold up yours." She flips her hair and goes to her third-row seat.

As soon as we're all sitting down and Mr. L starts talking, a note lands on my desk.

> What do you and that no-good soon-to-be fired team captain have in common?

I feel that bite like I'm bad. I feel bad. But, I tell myself, it'll all be over soon. I've just got to hold it together and we'll all be happy. Just as long as Marta doesn't find out. I write on the back of it:

> You. They want you off the team. You have to keep your mouth shut, all right? No matter what, do not tell them a thing.

That much is true. And I send it over. Mr. L catches me. "Charlie. Do you need to stay after school?"

"No, no, please, I'm sorry Mr. L." I slide down my seat and keep my eyes on him alone. It's getting tricky.

When the bell rings, I pull Marta into the bathroom to really drive the point home. "Tell Coach to keep his mouth shut too, all right? I know Pickler's not talking because he doesn't want anyone to know he's paying for it out of school funds. But Coach has a big mouth."

Marta looks at me with suspicion. "Are you up to something else?"

I take her shoulders in my hands and squeeze. "Have I ever let you down?"

"No, but—"

"But what?"

Marta pushes me back. "Don't you ever, and I mean ever, play me. Because if you do—"

I stop her right there. "Do you want to go to the JOs?"

Marta nods.

"Then tell Coach to keep his mouth shut. As soon as I know it's safe, I'll tell you. Until then, zip it."

"All right," she says.

Later that night after I get home from work, after my hot bath and bowl of orecchiette with mini chicken meatballs in a cream sauce, I sit in bed, staring at the dark screen of my laptop. I want to check in on Bobby but feel like it'll come off as slightly stalkerish.

I roll on my side. I'm in serious pain. I can barely move my arms, they're so tired from the lifting, and my gifted fingers are blistered. But I have almost one hundred dollars in my pocket. It's called tips, baby. That's a heck of a lot of money. Suddenly I don't feel so sorry for Richie and Marcos anymore; they're reeling it in. By the time I graduate from high school, they're going to be richer than Bill Gates.

I call Jai, but there's no answer on his end. Which is a good thing. Jai can see right through me, remember? The door opens, and Pen comes limping in and collapses on the bed.

"Why don't people care?" She pounds her pillow. "They're living creatures, after all."

"They are rodents, Pen."

"And rodents don't have hearts and souls?" she yells into the room.

Blueberry Pancakes = World Peace

When the alarm buzzes at six the next morning, I run and lock myself in the bathroom to prepare for my big, and I mean huge, day. The stress is killing me. Today I'm going for a pair of skinny vintage drop-crotch black sweatpants I got from this funky shop on La Brea back when my life was simpler. I add a white tank and a Kurt Cobain plaid shirt tied around the waist. Maybe Bobby and I could hang out at lunch. I'm teasing my hair to a perfect Seattle grunge mess when the most glorious smell comes in under the door.

Blueberry pancakes. I can literally smell them from the bathroom—the browning butter, cake, and berries. I jump the entire staircase like Wonder Woman and grab a plate.

Dad looks up from the screen. "Ever since they ran that

story about you in the tunnels, people are going crazy over the canyons. It's gonna implode. Your sister's right."

"Dear Lord, don't tell her that."

Pen comes bouncing down the steps. It pains me just how much she doesn't care about her looks. Today she's got her hair pulled back in a super tight bun. She looks like she could fly with those ears.

I scarf the last pancake and guzzle the juice while trying to visually measure the wingspan of each ear.

"The canyons could become the next Beverly Hills if we're not careful," Dad leans over and whispers to Pen. "It's a good thing, what you're doing."

I watch Mom flip the last batch—my batch. "Saving the world one rat at a time, right, Pen?" I burp. "Sorry."

Mom gives me the look. She drops two more tiny pancakes on my plate. "No more. And be nice."

"It's all right." Pen gives me the look. "She lives to be destructive. I live to be constructive. That's the difference between Charlie and me."

"Yes, Pen, you'll end up in the White House, and I'll end up in the jailhouse." I tap her on the head as I walk past.

"Oh, stop it, you two." Mom looks like she wants to hit me with the spatula.

"That's right, blame me." I look at Pen. "Perfectionism is a form of sibling abuse too, you know."

Everyone laughs. Why are they laughing? "It's true. Dr.

72

Scales told me." I stand my ground.

Felix comes dragging in. His blond hair is a mess. It's sticking up all over the place, and he's a wreck. His socks don't match. His pants hit his ankles like he's working in the sewers. "I'm starving." He sneezes and snot shoots out.

Suddenly it all makes sense. Dad's got on Tevas, Mom's wearing her orange Crocs. Pen looks like something out of a horror movie, and my little brother looks like he was dressed by the blind. "Mom, be honest. I was switched at birth, wasn't I?"

"No such luck." Mom hands Felix his plate of pancakes. Nothing throws her off.

"It's okay, you don't have to tell me right now." I take one more look at their fashion disasters. "Later.".

I leave early for school in the hope of "accidentally" running into Bobby. But the classroom is empty except for Mr. L, sipping his spicy tea, listening to his whales.

"Morning, Mr. L." I take a seat.

Bobby walks in seconds later. My heart leaps. Yay!

He tosses his backpack against the wall and falls into his seat. He looks mad.

"Hey." I act like I don't see him. Playing it cool.

He pulls up his hood and opens his art book to a page filled with lots of dead people, shot-out houses, and broken glass. He goes back to drawing.

I take a better look. Looks like two people covered in blood. These are not the pictures of a happy kid. "What's that?"

He turns the page. "A murder."

"Great. Fantastic." I pick up my book, *The Catcher in the Rye*. Holden Caulfield is positively optimistic compared to Bobby Brown.

The door hits the wall. Marta comes storming through, wheeling her pink roller backpack, hitting everything in sight. "Charlie!" She looks like she's about to explode. "You're never gonna believe this." She throws her roller backpack against the wall and comes stomping over. Her face is bright red, her eyes huge. But worst of all, she's got her hair in two ponytails.

She's dripping wet. "Please tell me that's water."

"Sweat." She wipes it with the back of her hand and licks it. "Yeah. Sweat. I've already put in three hours at the gym."

I cringe. "Nasty."

But Marta doesn't care. She jumps up and down. "You're not listening to me."

Whatever it is, I don't want to hear it. All I want is for Marta to be quiet. To not speak until after I book my job.

"Pickler," she yells at the top of her lungs, "just handed me my confirmed ticket and entrance number to the Junior Olympics in Texas!! He did it. I'm in."

SHUT UP! I mouth.

"What?" Bobby looks up. People are beginning to walk in.

"Nothing, nothing at all." I scan the room. So far none of

Lillian's crew is here. "Marta, shut the heck up!" I grab her by the arms and impale her with the evil in my eyes. "You're not supposed to say a word, remember?"

But Marta won't stop. "I, Marta Urloff, am going to Texas to compete in a Junior Olympics championship meet!" she screams into the room. "And no one can stop me."

"Congrats, Marta." Bobby tries to sound happy.

But me, I'm beginning to panic. "If they hear you, we're done."

"Why?" She throws her hands up. "They can't do a thing to me. You said it yourself. I have the ticket."

Oh, but they can do something to me.

Bobby's listening, catching on. "What's up with you, Coop?"

I ignore him. If I can just contain her before they walk in, maybe, just maybe, not all is lost.

Marta keeps going full speed ahead. "Coach is putting me in first position. Do you know what this means? Take that, Lillian! Ha!"

What it means is my life is about to be ruined. "Marta, please shut your mouth."

"But why?" Bobby looks suspicious now too. "She's got the ticket. There's nothing they can do to her now."

If he only knew.

Marta falls into her chair. She drops her head way back. I can see up her nostrils. "He believes I have what it takes to go all the way to the Olympics." She pounds her feet on the floor.

Mr. L turns his attention to Marta. He throws up his hands. "Everyone, stop what you're doing."

Oh, no. That's it. It's over.

Mr. L claps. "Marta is going to represent Happy Canyon at the upcoming Junior Olympics in Texas!"

"Yeah, Marta!" The whole classroom's jumping up and down. And me, I just sit back and wait for the you-know-what to hit.

Bobby nudges me. "What's with you?"

My eyes are on the clock. The final bell is just about to ring. One minute left. I'm doomed. There is no way Lillian's *not* going to find out.

Bobby grins. "They're here."

Lillian and Erica are standing silently in front of the class. Lillian takes one look at the crowd surrounding Marta and she knows. "What's going on?" Lillian says.

I'm about to get my butt kicked.

"Coach just told her the school's picking up the tab." Bobby rubs it in hard.

"Tab for what?" Lillian wants it spelled out.

"The JOs." Bobby beams. "She's his number one star pick."

Lillian's head swivels until her eyes lock onto me. "Is that right?"

I slide off my chair. I want to hide.

Marta slaps my desk. "Without the help of my best friend over here, I never could have done it."

76

"I didn't do anything," I mumble weakly.

"Charlie, huh?" Lillian is as cold as snow.

Mr. L beams with pride. "Class, I have to step out for just a second. Get your books."

They wait for the door to close before they pounce. It's going down, right now. I pick up my book and hide my face. It's gonna hurt.

Behind me, I hear Lillian whisper, "You're dead."

My heart pounds hard in my chest.

Erica gets up and comes over to our desks. I can see it in her eyes. She's teasing me, circling like a vulture. Erica stops right in front of us. She leans down and glares.

But Marta feels untouchable. "You guys better be nice to me and Charlie or I'm gonna talk to Coach. I'm already team captain in Texas."

Lillian's face turns purple. "I'm team captain."

"Not anymore." Marta's loving it.

Marta, shut up. Please just shut up.

Lillian takes one of those deep scary cleansing breaths, leans forward so she's in Marta's face, and says, "What if"—she braids her hair casually, like this is all fun and games—"I was to tell you that you'll pull out of the JOs all by yourself?"

"You're insane." Marta waves her away, laughing. "Nothing's gonna take me away from the JOs."

"Mark my words," Lillian sings softly.

The door opens. Mr. L claps loudly. "Class, time to quiet

down. We have a lot of ground to cover."

I can barely breathe. When is she going to rat me out to Marta? How's it going to go down? In public, in private? In pieces? Or all at once? I'm so stressed I'm eating my fingers. Mr. L turns his back to us and begins to write on the board.

And then, toward the end of class, it happens. Two paper airplanes fly from the back of the room, up through the air. One lands on Bobby's desk. The other on Marta's desk. Bobby looks at it with dread. Like he knows it's bad news. Marta looks at it like a foreign object—it's probably the first time she's ever had a note passed to her and not at her. I watch her unfold it first. She reads it. Slowly, her eyes fill with tears. Bobby reads his. His eyes fill with hate.

The snack bell rings. I'm done.

I'm So Not a Scorpion

I run after them both. But Bobby is gone before I even make it out of the classroom. The hallway is already crammed with kids pushing and shoving their way to get through the dang doors and out to freedom. I tap Marta on the shoulder just as she reaches the doors. "I need to talk to you."

She turns long enough to show me her fangs. "How could you?" She runs down the stairs.

I run faster. "What was in that note?"

She goes straight to the spot we eat lunch in, sits down, and opens up her stained unicorn lunch box she's had since she was three. "The note?" She reaches into her backpack, takes it out, and reads:

Marta,

Thought you should know. Charlie's working at the Patch to make money for head shots for a TV show about gymnastics. Chad wanted you to try out, too, but she told him that you couldn't do gymnastics. And you hated TV. She's not your friend. She never was. Don't trust her.

Your friends and teammates,
Lillian and Erica.

P.S. I can get you an audition.

She folds the note into a tight square and puts it back in her backpack. She takes out her sandwich and says nothing.

My hands are trembling. "Marta, please, let me explain."

But Marta's as still as stone. "It's already been explained."

Bobby throws the ball *at* me. It hits me hard in the leg.

I look at him, at her. I have to make a choice—what docs call triage the situation. Bobby, he's just plain disappointed. I can handle that. But Marta, she's the kind of person who will destroy an entire town to get back at me. So I choose Marta.

"Marta," I say calmly, "listen to me. I was going to tell him to look for something for you. This part is for a kid who *can't* do gymnastics. She's pathetic, a total loser. So not you." Okay, I was laying it on a little thick, but I was fighting for my life in more ways than one.

She shakes her head. Her eyes are red and disgusted. "Then why'd you lie?"

"Yo, Cooper!" Bobby throws the ball at me again. It hits me in the butt this time. "We're done."

"What?" I turn.

He shakes his head and spits.

"Bobby, come on!" I throw up my arms.

He spits again. "Done." He pulls up his hood, turns away, and is gone.

I'll deal with him later. I turn back to Marta. "Marta." I take a deep breath. "You have your thing. Come on, this is my thing."

Marta nods like she agrees. She takes a bite of her sandwich and looks up at the swaying bamboo. For a second I think I've gotten through to her. And then she starts. "You ever heard of the scorpion and the frog story?"

"Nope." No offense, but I don't want to hear a story. I just want to move on. I get up, walk around, change the flow of energy a little. "Hey, did you tell Greta about the JOs? She has to be so happy for you! And what was that supposed to mean back there when Lillian said you'll drop out yourself, huh? That was weird, right?"

But Marta just looks straight ahead. "It was one of my mother's favorites—"

I try to stop her, but she steamrolls right over me.

"One day, a scorpion decides he wants to live across the river. But he can't swim and has no way of getting across. He sees a frog sitting there and decides to ask for help."

"Charlie!"

I hear my name. Thank God. I look up. Pen's waving. "Come here. Felix wants you."

Marta grabs my hand.

"Marta, please." I know where this is going. I can see it in her eyes. Marta has not forgiven. Marta has not moved on. Marta is pissed.

"You know what the frog says, right?" She keeps going like I have no choice. " 'How do I know that if I help you, you won't try to kill me?' "

" 'Because,' " the scorpion replies, " 'if I try to kill you, then I would die, too. I cannot swim.' "

"Exactly." I grab her wrists. "I don't want to kill you, Marta. I want you to be successful. Would I ever have run away, hidden in the tunnels, faked your aunt's visa, risked everything, if I only ever thought about myself?"

But she doesn't care. Marta keeps at it like a slow-moving train headed for disaster. "The frog asks, 'How do I know you won't just wait till we get to the other side and *then* kill me?' "

From across the yard, Lillian and Erica have been watching. After a few minutes, they stroll over and take a seat behind Marta, like this is story hour.

I glare at them. "Go away."

"No, stay," Marta says calmly. Is she blind or what?

"Oh, they're your friends now?" I laugh. "Please! They'll sell you out the second they have a chance."

"'Because,' promises the scorpion, 'once you've taken me to the other side of this river, I will be so grateful for your help, I would never hurt you.'"

Erica reaches into her bag of chips. "Hey, guys," Erica yells into the yard. "Marta's telling a story about Charlie. It's a good one. Come on over!"

Kids start coming over—fourth, fifth, and sixth graders. Before I know it, the Losers Lunch area is full. Everyone is listening. Sweat drips down my back. I can feel it. I'm going down in flames. Marta waits for everyone to sit. "Can't we just talk about this in private, please?"

But Marta is no longer talking directly to me. "So"—she swallows—"the frog takes the scorpion across the river on his back. He even stays near the surface so the scorpion won't drown. And then, halfway across the river, the frog suddenly feels a sharp sting in his back and, out of the corner of his eye, he sees the scorpion remove his stinger from the frog's back.

"'You fool!'" croaks the dying frog. "'Now we shall both die! Why on earth did you do that?'

"The scorpion shrugs. 'It is my nature,' says the scorpion. 'I cannot help myself.' And they both sink into the muddy waters of the river and die."

Marta's eyes are swimming in tears. "You, Charlie"—she jabs her finger in my chest—"are a scorpion, and you will never, ever change." Everyone claps.

Oh, give me a break! Seriously? "Is this not the worst case of exaggeration you've ever seen in your life?"

Silence.

"Have you forgotten that I saved you?" I stare at her, at them. "I put everything on the line to help you when no one else would."

Marta shakes her head. "I was an assignment. A project. That's all."

Lillian raises her hand like we're in class. "She did it to save herself."

Babette nods. "Her shrink told her to."

"Yes, it's true at the beginning, but I changed—" I back up. They're not listening. No one wants to know the truth. They just want to gang up on me. "I am no scorpion." Maybe a long time ago I had a little scorpion in me, but now I am good. I am kind.

"Well, looks like you changed back." Babette shrugs, and they all laugh.

"I got you the JOs. What more do you want?"

"To not lie," Marta says.

I look at all of them—it's them against me just like it's always been. And maybe how it will always be. Like they've never withheld a little info to help their chances. Please. Then I see Bobby in the back of the crowd. He's shaking his head, looking at me like I'm a piece of poo. I can't believe it—even Bobby.

"It was a white lie," I announce. "You're telling me you've never told one?" What liars. "You're all a bunch of hypocrites. You know that? I'm more honest than all of you put together."

That's when they start booing me.

"Get lost, scorpion!" they chant. The sound of their feet pounding on the metal picnic bench fills my brain. "Go! Go! Go!"

I move back as fast as I can without turning. They're moving toward me. No one stops them.

Their voices join together in a loud, mean song.

I turn and run as fast as I can. Up the stairs and into the only place I know they won't follow me—the library. I run through the doors like I'm on fire.

"Charlie?" Ms. Myrtle looks at me through these glasses that cover her entire face. "You okay?"

I wipe my eyes, my nose, and check the door. Phew—no one's coming. But I'm shaking like crazy. "I'm fine, Ms. Myrtle." I choke back the tears. Not a single person stood up for me. No one. I got her the JOs. Her dream on a silver platter. No one could have done that for her but me. I pull out a chair and type in the school's internet password. I only have a few minutes before the bell rings.

Hey Jai,
I don't know where you are, but I need you AS to the P. Email me back if you're there.

Send.
Next email:

Mom,
Please pick me up as early as you can today. I'll be waiting.
Charlie
P.S. It's been a really bad day.

And finally—and boy, is my heart beating for this one:

Hey, Chad, my man—
The head shots will be in your hands by tonight. I've been practicing all week for the audition and I'm ready to go. Call me as soon as you get them. I'm free anytime.
Charlie

I stare at the screen, waiting, just waiting for an answer from someone, somewhere out there in the world who still wants to talk to me. Certainly Chad of all people would understand my not wanting Marta in on the audition. He should even applaud my initiative.

A message comes up. It's Jai.

What's happening?

I type as fast as my fingers can move.

Where have you been? I've been going crazy trying to reach you.

I had to move, Charlie. It's been bad.

What do you mean bad?

Can't talk about it. More later. What's up?

Injustice.

Your middle name.

I'm talking burning-at-the-stake kind of injustice, Jai. Everyone hates me.

What happened?

I lied. It was a little lie.

It is not the size of the lie, Charlie. It is the size of the ripple the lie creates. Like a pebble in a pond.

Oh, please.

You must go and correct it.

Too late.

Never too late.

I hate you.

No, you don't.

The bell rings. I pretend not to notice. Ms. Myrtle looks over the cover of her book and says, "Time to go."

It feels like a death sentence. The last thing I want to do is leave this room and see anyone else at all. I quickly type:

> I got to go. I'll Skype you tonight.

I stand up.

"Ms. Cooper, class has started." Ms. Myrtle points at the door.

All I have to do is make it across to Mr. L's room without getting cornered.

Ms. Myrtle looks up at me again. "Ms. Cooper?"

"I'm going." I suck in my gut, take a deep breath. I crack open the door. Down the hall, some kids are scrambling into their rooms, but outside Mr. L's, the coast is clear. "On a count of one, two, three . . ." I run across the hall and into his room, where Mr. L's got his mating orca CD rolling in the classroom. But not even the orcas can calm my nerves. Everyone is staring at me like they can't believe I have the nerve to show my face. Even the kids who never have an idea of what's going on know what's going on.

Mr. L turns off the orcas. "Nice of you to come back." He goes back to his book. I slip into my chair between Bobby and Marta. They scoot their desks away like I stink. They ignore me like I am a ghost. "We're about to pick up *The Absolutely True Diary of a Part-Time Indian*. Can anyone tell us what's happening?" asks Mr. L.

Babs raises her hand. "Here Junior and his best friend have a massive fight. His best friend tells him he's a traitor and Junior leaves the school." She nods. "Which is really a great idea, don't ya think, Charlie?"

Everyone laughs.

When the lunch bell rings, I grab my backpack and pretend to search for something. I'm not going anywhere. Not a chance. As long as Mr. L is in here, I'm safe. Kids start walking out. I keep my head low. As they pass, I feel them hit, kick my chair. I say nothing.

A ball narrowly misses hitting me in the head. Bobby again.

Bobby shakes his head in disgust. "I can't believe you did that, Cooper."

I look up. "What did I do, exactly?"

"Sold Marta out."

I gulp the desk. "She wouldn't even have time to do it, Bobby! Come on, seriously."

"Then you shouldn't have lied." He takes the ball and starts bouncing it against the wall.

Yeah, yeah, yeah. Everyone's perfect but me.

I see Marta leaving with Lillian and Erica, like they're buddies. Bobby's friends are waiting at the door, staring at him. But he's not done with me yet. "Just so you know, Lillian and Erica took a picture of the note and put it on Instagram. Everyone knows. Probably even that agent dude you lied to knows."

His friends wave to him. "Good luck with that, Cooper."

Great. Thanks. I wait for everyone to leave before I get up and look out the window. Wouldn't you know, Marta's at the popular table. They're all laughing together like one big happy family. I put my face to the glass and watch them, every detail of them. The way they huddle around her, treat her like a princess. What are they up to? They hate her more than they hate me. This can't be the end of their plan. There has to be a phase two. And then I remember that thing Lillian said: "What if I was to tell you that you'd pull out of the JOs all by yourself?"

"What does that mean?" I hit my head against the glass. "What are they planning?"

Mr. L clears his throat. "You dining in today, Ms. Cooper?"

"I think I need a permanent reservation, Mr. L." I hit my head again.

Run, Run
as Fast as You Can

The worst day of my life is finally over.

It's 2:40. Since lunch, I've been staring at the clock like I'm in open-heart surgery. Swear to God. For the last hour, during silent reading, my eyes have been on that clock. My legs are cramped in a half squat. The second the bell rings, my plan is to:

- Run like hell down the stairs, through the upper yard, and out into the parking lot.
- Locate the old Volvo and jump in before anyone can see me, heckle me, or tell my mother what happened today.

The bell rings. I launch myself out of the classroom. I don't even look back. I don't even attempt to talk to Marta or Bobby, because nothing I say will change a thing. I race down the steps, through the totally empty upper yard, and make it out the door. The buses have already pulled into the parking lot, which means it's blocked. My mother could not have parked here. There's only one other place she'd be. I run down the street and find her at the lower end of the school, sitting in her parked Volvo, reading. I yank open the door. "Let's go!"

"Whoa, where did you come from?" Mom looks at me like I'm crazy.

"Gotta go, gotta go, gotta go!" I glance up at the lower playground and hope that no one comes to the gate and says something I'm going to have to explain. Like Pen, for example.

"What about your brother and sister?" She glances at the playground.

"They're staying." My foot is tapping. I'm about to explode.

She looks over at me like she's examining me. "Charlie?"

TRUE FACT: Mom's got X-ray vision.

I take a deep breath. "She's doing the dead-squirrel meeting, Mom, remember?" I try to calm myself, but it's hard. I'm freaking out. "She's walking home with Felix later. We have to go."

"It's the Save the Wildlife Corridor meeting, and it's about a lot more than dead squirrels, Charlie, so be nice."

I steady my tapping foot. "Sorry."

Slowly Mom turns on the car. It chugs to life. I drop lower

92

into my seat. Please, please, let's just get out of here. I'm scared to death Pen's hairy-mustache face will suddenly appear and Mom will stop. But lucky for me, we leave without seeing her and head down the road. Mom gets ready to turn right onto Laurel Canyon.

"I got your email," she says without looking at me. "Did something happen today?"

"No," I say. "Just really excited."

"It's exciting." Her hands grip the wheel tighter.

"I think we should cancel the Halloween party," I announce with the utmost certainty.

She turns off NPR and looks at me. "Is that so?"

"I'm super broken up about it"—not—"but I'm a little over whelmed with all that's going on." I can see her staring at me, like an alien has invaded my body, so I add, "Dr. Scales said to keep an eye on that."

She's stunned. "But you love Halloween more than any other day of the year."

"I know."

"And this year we're on the Houdini estate. It doesn't get any better."

Not when you have zero friends. No, worse, I have negative friends, because I have enemies. People who want me gone.

She's still struggling. "Wanna tell me what's really going on?"

"Nothing, I swear, just no time. And Pen's so into her Save

the Corridor thing." I shrug. "I think we should just have a little family party—"

Mom gets this weird look on her face. "Family party?"

"Yeah, and some trick-or-treaters, but nothing big. No invitations. Just some good family time, Mom."

"All right, well . . . it's this weekend," she says, still surprised. "But I'll talk to Dad, Pen, and Felix. It's fine with me."

"Thanks, Mom." No way would I suffer a boycotted Halloween party. No way would I stand there watching *no one* arrive. I check out the Country Store on our left, and feel my nerves smooth as we get farther and farther away from the horror that is my life.

Mom starts nodding like she's just figured it out. "I think it's smart of you not to do too much. You're taking care of you, and that's good." She rubs my knee, turns up NPR, and thankfully says nothing for the rest of the way.

Fifteen minutes later, we pull up to the photography studio. It's on Sunset Boulevard, of course. "All right." She grins like it's a defining moment. "This is it. I called him before we left. He's expecting you." She turns off the engine. "I'll be right here."

I open my bag, pull out my MAC Rock and Roll lip crayon, apply it in the broken mirror. Then I tease my hair. I paint my nails black with whatever Sharpie I can find.

I throw my arms around her and hug her. "Thanks, Mom." I'm nervous as heck, but there's no place I'd rather be. This is it. A new beginning. A new me. I so have to nail this. During this hour, I have to make sure all aspects of my personality are captured so that there is no way the producers can say no. I get out, tie the shirt around my waist, and kiss my mom one more time. I take a massive cleansing breath and walk through the door. To new beginnings.

My First Photo Shoot

It's so dark in here, my eyes burn. But slowly, the details emerge. The black lobby is covered in photographs of Hollywood stars. I go up to their pictures to check it out, but the closer I get, the more I notice that most of them are in black-and-white, which, of course, means that these stars are all probably dead. The guy should seriously consider taking them down and putting up color pictures.

The door opens. A small man comes out. He's got a huge orange afro and matching curly beard that looks like it's attacking his face. And he's got all these weird, broken yellow teeth. He's wearing a dress with a scarf and slippers. He's looking at me in a way I don't understand. He's coming near me. I ball up both fists, ready to punch.

"Perfection! You must be Charlie!" He puts his hands together like he's praying. "Chad told me—he told me. Divine, you are divine." He closes his eyes for a really long time, then announces, "I am Morris the Great. Come, come into my studio. Let me study you." I follow him inside. The place is like a tomb, black, cold as a fridge. For a second I want to get my mom. "Chad told me," he squeals, "but I had no idea!"

I peel off my clothes to reveal the truly remarkable black-and-rhinestone leotard that I have underneath my pants. It's both shiny and scaly at the same time, and it actually sucks in my stomach for me.

"Stand there." He points. "Perfect! Fantastic!" He starts to click. "Now, do some moves."

I freeze. "Moves?"

"Think gymnast. Think, I'm clawing my way to the top."

Right. I touch the sequins on my top and I concentrate. What do I want to show Chad most of all?

That I can look like a gymnast.

That I can look evil and cute while doing it.

First I do cartwheels, splits, and back bends. Thanks to Marta, they're pretty dang good.

"Impressive!"

He snaps away for an hour. "Awesome!" I do as many cutthroat-sister looks as I can muster. Then I throw in some highly competitive glares by imagining just how much I hate Lillian.

"Punch!" he cries out. "Punch the air in front of you. You're a fighter, Charlie, a fighter."

"Lord, ain't that the truth." And so I punch. I kick. I karate chop until he's done clicking.

"Funny. Do funny," he commands. I run headfirst into the black wall and fall down. I am so in the zone that I don't even realize time has gone by until he falls like a giant lump of pumpkin goo onto the black carpet, rolls onto his stomach, and laughs.

I walk over and look at him. "Are you all right, mister?"

"All right?" He laughs. "That was the best photo shoot I've done since Depp. You are a beacon of light in this horribly bland, this mediocre world of falsehoods. You are truth, Charlie! Ah!" He rubs his face. "These are going to be out of this world."

I hold on to his every word. "So you think I'll get the job?"

"Oh, yes," he says, totally seriously. "Yes, I do."

"Please send them as fast as you can." I can't wait for Chad to get them! I can't wait for the next chapter of my life to begin. Good-bye, Happy Canyon. Hello, Hollywood! "Where can I pay?"

"Pay? You?" He jumps up, now drenched with sweat. "Never, never. Just let me put one on my wall. Let me be the one who says I discovered you, please."

All that pumpkin schlepping for nothing, the rotten insides, the goo. I want to kill my mother.

Mr. Morris the Great walks me to the door and turns the sign to read CLOSED. "I'm downloading your images for the rest of the day. I cannot let anything else enter into my visual field, just you."

He opens the door and shields his eyes. "You're a star, Charlie Cooper, a star."

I emerge onto the Sunset Strip a new woman. Mom's Volvo is right there. I practically throw myself into the car. "Mom!" I grab her.

She jumps. "What? What?"

"First of all," I point out immediately, "I don't even have to pay."

"What do you mean?" She puts on her glasses and looks me over. "Why don't you have to pay?"

"He said I was so amazing, so gifted, so perfect, he was happy to do it for free as long as I let him put up a picture on his wall, and believe me, he needs a little color up there."

"So it went well?"

"Well?" I'm out of my mind. "It was amazing! Phenomenal, fun. Did I say amazing?" I can barely contain myself. I don't recall ever being this happy in my whole entire life. "Now I know I was born to do this." I look up at the billboards and see my face up there.

Mom kisses me. "You hungry?"

"Starved." Pumped. I'm on the brink, I can feel it.

Mom pulls a U-turn on Sunset. "How about we grab something to eat before you go to work?"

Whoa, whoa, put the brakes on, lady. "Didn't you hear me? The pictures are free. Free, as in no more slave labor."

Mom puts on her lip gloss. "But they're counting on you to come today, Charlie."

I can't even believe she's saying this. "You're kidding me, right?"

"Wrong." She pulls her hair into a loose ponytail.

I'm about to argue when I realize that the longer I stay away from home, the longer I can put off answering any questions about what happened today at school. "But I get McDonald's, all right?"

"That's not real food." Her voice gets all low. "But"—she squeezes my knee—"as a special celebration. I'm so proud of you."

TRUE FACT: When I'm rich and famous, I'm eating McDonald's every day.

I stare at myself in the side mirror, suddenly seeing everything that he saw. My playfulness, my serious jawline, wise eyes, mischievous smile. "He said I'm a natural." Me, C.C. Cooper. Maybe I'll change my name to just C.C.

We drive for a while. I'm lost in my world, putting my middle-school past behind me and thinking of my future, when Mom breaks the silence. "Pen called while you were in there." She drops it like that.

I curse the day she got a cell phone.

"She said something about you having a tough day at school today. Is that right?"

Great, Pen knows. Of course she knows; everyone in the entire school, canyon, and possibly the city of Los Angeles probably knows. "Kinda." I turn away from her. "Do we really have to talk about it?"

"No." Mom shakes her head. "We don't."

Thank God she learned about parental boundaries at Dr. Scales's office. She drives down Sunset Boulevard for a few minutes without saying a word, and I think I'm off the hook.

Then she says, "Is this why you want to cancel the Halloween party?"

Clearly she'd forgotten the boundary talk. "No, no, Mom."

"If you need to, we can talk to Dr. Scales." She points to where his office is. "I'm sure he'd love to see you."

TRUE FACT: This is called blackmail. Plain and simple.

I look over at her. I can see the vein throbbing in the middle of her forehead. "It's nothing, Mom, no big deal, all right?" I shift my leg so I am practically on the door.

"According to your sister, they're calling you the scorpion at school." She's got that concerned look. "Doesn't sound like a compliment."

"Well, you're wrong." I pull my legs under me. "Didn't you know scorpions symbolize luck? And the moms carry their babies on their backs," I explain. "They're actually supernice little animals."

She turns. Her left eyebrow is up like a giant question mark. "Really?"

"Okay, fine!" I yell. "I told a lie, all right?" I slap my thigh. "I didn't want Marta to audition for this stupid part, so I told a lie. And now it's coming back and biting me on the butt, big-time." I turn to the window to avoid her look of total disappointment.

We're stalled in traffic. Mom's voice is strangely calm. "So what are you gonna do about it?"

"I already got Pickler to pay for Marta's flight to the JOs, which is her dream, by the way." She says nothing, just shakes her head. "I didn't buy her off!" I yell. "I got her the Junior Olympics—"

"But"—she stops me—"you did it because you, Charlie, wanted her to stay away from the audition. That's called manipulation."

"I know."

"And it's wrong."

"I know." But guess what. This is my destiny, and there's nothing Lillian can do to stop it.

Shut Pen Up

Mom pulls into our driveway.

The car comes to a stop. "Be careful." Mom turns off the ignition and we sit there in the creaking old Volvo under a sky of stars.

I look up at the house. I say a silent prayer that Pen isn't waiting for us downstairs. I see Houdini looking at me from up above, perched on the mountain, and feel sad. "You don't know what it's like for me."

She shakes her head. It's so still in the car. "You're right, I don't. But I do know it's the same everywhere you go."

"Say what?"

"Because it's inside you, Charlie," she says. "The craziness that follows you is *in* you."

"Great, thanks a lot." I kick open the car door, about to leave, when she touches my back.

"Don't you see?" Her voice is soft but has a heaviness to it. "Hollywood, Happy Canyon, it doesn't matter where you go—"

But this is too much. "I have to go." I grab my stuff and run.

"Charlie!"

But I don't want to listen. I run through the door and drop my backpack in the middle of the floor the second I get in. The kitchen is empty. Mom comes in behind me, balancing bags from the market on her hips. I'm about to launch myself up the stairs when Mom announces,

"Stop right there."

I turn. Mom's pointing to my backpack, and she's turning red. She hands it to me. "Put it away, Charlie."

"Fine." I climb the stairs. All I want is a quiet space and my laptop. I throw open my door, about to launch myself onto my bed, when Pen spins around. She's at her desk in her pj's, doing homework. "I stood up for you." She hisses like she's been waiting hours for this. "I even told Lillian you had Marta's back. Jesus, Charlie, when, when will you ever change?"

Felix is on his bed, reading a comic book. He puts it down and asks, "Is that why everyone hates you again, Charlie?"

I grab my laptop. "No more lectures, all right?" I take a deep breath and turn on my machine. "Plus, if you really want to know, I got her into the Junior Olympics. I was the one who got Pickler to pay for it. Me."

105

Pen looks almost speechless. "Then why are they all saying you're a scorpion?" She taps her pencil. "You're lying."

"Don't you get what this is all about?" I stare at her. "It's pretty simple, Pen. They want her out of the JOs. Lillian promised me if I kept her out, she'd leave me alone. But I didn't. I did the so-called right thing and got Pickler to pay for Marta. And now they're making me pay."

For the moment, Pen's silent, which is great, because all I want is to hear from Chad and book the job. I open my email and scan as fast as I can. If he hasn't written, I swear to God I'm going over there by bus. But there's nothing there. Not a peep. Is it possible he's seen the note Lillian posted on Instagram and now wants nothing to do with me? I'm freaking out. Morris said they were perfect. What's happening?

"Charlie!" Dad yells up. "Come down here, please."

I look up at Pen. "Did you tell him?"

She shakes her head. "Not yet."

I almost can't believe it. "Why not?"

"I wanted to see if you'd have the guts to tell them yourself." She folds her arms like she's my mother. I feel like throwing my pillow at her face. I close the computer. "For your information, I already told Mom and will tell Dad myself." I slam the door and run down the stairs.

Dad's standing there slapping the phone against his hand. He's not laughing. I'm getting a bad feeling. "What's wrong, Dad?"

106

He shakes his head. "This has to be the twentieth time that pain in the butt, Chad, has called." The phone's in his hand, and he looks like he wants to kill it. He hands it to me. "Tell him once is enough."

My jaw drops. I take a calm breath. I don't want to sound overeager. Desperate. I take the phone. "Hey Chad, how are ya?" I ask casually, though my heart is pounding.

"I got your head shots." His voice sounds so dead. Like he, like he hates them.

"Do you . . ." I start to panic. I don't know what to say. "Well, do you like them?"

"Like them?" he squeals. "I don't like them. I love them. I want to marry them. I want to gaze at them like fat American tourists gaze at the *Mona Lisa*."

So he doesn't know about Marta.

He clears his throat, his voice gets real smooth, and then he says, "And my dear girl, it's not just me who likes them. The people at ABC Family love them. They want you to know you're their number-one pick for the part."

"Really?" I turn and whisper. I'm freaking out. I can't hide how happy I am, how relieved I am. "Seriously, their first pick?"

"They're drooling, baby. They see star written all over you. Those shots are beyond fab. They're epic."

"Get the heck out of here!" I squeal. Dad gives me a look. I know that look. That's the don't-get-too-excited-because-your-heart's-going-to-get-snapped-into-little-pieces look.

"It's your realness, Cooper. Plain and simple." It rolls off his tongue so quickly it sounds like a line he gives to everyone. "They like that you don't care about your looks. They like that you are not bothered by your weight. And, and . . ." He's laughing. "Get this, they love, love, love your fashion. Apparently the character they want you to play has an equally quirky fashion sense."

"I've been making up my own designs since I was three."

Dead silence.

"Since I was three," I repeat.

"So," Chad says, "there's only two things left. How's your acting?"

I stare at myself in the window. "Ever heard of Meryl Streep?"

"Misplaced confidence. I love it!" he yells. "I'm messengering over a scene from one of their scripts for you to read on camera. Practice with a friend so you're all set for the audition."

I don't have any friends.

"And your gymnastics. You have your routine down?"

"Absolutely." I do a stretch in front of the mirror.

"How bad do you want this?" he asks.

Is he taunting me? "I want it more than anything else in the world," I say with complete honesty.

"Then you're the right girl for the part," he says. "Practice your lines. I'll call you Monday."

The doorbell rings. "Charlie!" Dad calls me. I can tell he's beginning to get mad. "You're needed for a signature."

I run for it.

A signature? I peek through the door to see a man in black leather, black helmet, holding a seriously thick manila envelope. He hands me a pen. I don't even have a signature yet, so I just kinda pretend to have a super-fancy cursive signature. Note to self: start practicing autograph. The man hands me the huge pack and hops on his bike. "Cool pad you got here," he says to me like it's mine. I see my dad's face and can't really tell what he's thinking, but he's thinking of something, all right. On the package it says my name, typed, and above it there's a big CONFIDENTIAL. I rub my hands over it. It feels so real, like it's already mine.

"Is this for your audition?" Dad leans in.

I throw my arms around him. My middle-school horror is lessening by the second. "If I can get this show, Dad, we'll buy this place."

He squeezes me tight and kisses the top of my head. "You're a thoughtful girl, Charlie, no matter what they say."

Destiny Comes Early

The call comes early on Monday morning. I trip over a few hundred stuffed animals, wipe the drool from my lips, the sleep from my eyes. I run down the stairs, grab the phone, and clear my throat.

"Hello?" my voice croaks.

"Good morning, Superstar!" Chad's had a few espressos.

Suddenly I'm wide-awake. I open the fridge, hunt down some leftover Domino's, and eat it cold, like a little slice of heaven.

"I need you to come in this morning," he says. "The good people at ABC Family want to talk to you in person, pronto. You took a look at the script I sent?"

"A look? Are you kidding me? I memorized every word." I peek out the window. The sun is lifting over the canyon. Today's the day—I can feel it.

"There's loads of money on the table. So don't choke."

"Define *loads*." If I get this, Mom and Dad can sell that Volvo and buy more meat.

"Five grand a week. Give or take."

I hold on to the fridge. "Five grand as in thousand, as in five of those thousands every seven days, as in twenty of them a month?"

"They're casting the show this week. They'll start rehearsing the pilot a week from today and will shoot it in two weeks. If the pilot goes well, the network will order a full fifteen episodes—you following?"

I can hardly believe I'm having this conversation. God, I love the sound of that—shooting the pilot!

"They think you're perfect and I'm pretty sure I can close this, but dang it, Charlie, you've got to nail the audition. I'll send a car to your school at ten." He hangs up.

I run back upstairs to change. Pen's in the bathroom and Felix is putting both legs in one pant hole on his bed.

I pull them off and hand them back. "Two legs, two holes." I put on fishnets, then the leotard I wore for the photo shoot, and my tutu, and slip on a pair of Converses. Pen comes out, I run into the bathroom, lock the door. Brush teeth, slap on some deodorant, and then I take a moment. I study my face in the mirror.

This is what I know:

- This is the last time I will feel like a loser.
- This is the last time I will send out an invitation and have zero responses.
- This is the last time I will ever, and I mean ever, have to eat in a classroom or a library or a bathroom stall.
- This is the last time I will be defined by what *they* think of me.

There's a knock. "I'm gonna pee all over you if you don't open up."

I open the door. Felix is still half asleep. His pants are around his ankles. His hands are cupping his privates. He runs past me for the toilet. I close the door.

Mom calls out, "You guys want bagels?"

I head downstairs and pull out a chair next to Pen. "Bagels sound great."

Mom's in her nightgown. "My alarm didn't go off and I'm late, late, late." She runs to my backpack. "Do you have lunch?"

"I did them last night, Mom," Pen says. "Felix gets hot dogs. Charlie pizza, Fruit Roll-Ups, apple slices—"

"Whoa! Stop right there."

Is there anything worse than your sister making your lunch

for you? "Don't do my lunch!" I yell at her. "I hate when you pack our lunches." I look in mine. "I hate apples, hate Fruit Roll-Ups, and the pizza—by the time it's lunch, it's disgusting. Mom, please."

Pen throws my lunch box at me. I say nothing for fear she'll open her hairy lips.

I leave it there. "Anyway, I have to get to Chad's this morning for the audition. It's an emergency."

"An emergency?" Her eyebrow lifts up.

"The producers want to see me now. It's do or die."

Pen shakes her head.

I want to stab her with a butter knife. "Pen. Can you either mind your own business, or get your own dang life?"

"My life is you, Charlie. Don't you know that by now?" She squeezes my shoulder. The urge to strangle her is overwhelming.

"What time does he want to see you?"

"At eleven." I ready myself for her usual speech about missing school.

Of course Mom's already shaking her head. "Um, well . . ." She winces as she goes through her day in her head. "Your dad and I both have an appointment. I can't get out of it. Can we do it at lunch?"

"Chad says he'll send a car." I have to count to ten to stop myself from exploding at the thought of it. I hope it's a limo. And more importantly, I hope everyone in the entire school will be there to watch me get into it.

"A car?" Mom immediately doesn't like the idea. "Oh"—long sigh—"I don't know about that."

"I'll call you the second they pick me up. And I'll have Chad email you the contracts to look at."

Pen cocks her head again. "Isn't that a little premature?"

"No." I grab Mom's arm and pull her away from my annoying, nosy-as-heck sister. "Please, Mom, please!"

The room is silent. Mom's shaking her head. The clock's ticking—it doesn't look good. I'm about to plead when suddenly Pen says, "Mom, if she gets the show, she'll be in a car all the time," Pen says. "It's totally normal."

Say what? I shake my head. Why is she suddenly helping me? Pen keeps at her, stating my case until Mom starts nodding like Pen's making a whole lot of sense. And then she says the magic word: "Fine. But call us when you get there." And then she launches into "Tell Chad this will not happen again, you hear me? School is the most important thing." Mom pecks me on the cheek. "I'll have my cell phone with me all the time, okay, baby?"

"Okay, Mom." I give her a big kiss.

"School, Charlie. Now."

"Just one thing." I run into the living room for a quick check of all my favorite sites. But Mom follows me. She takes one look at the screen.

"Oh, please! Not at eight in the morning!" She gasps like

I'm looking at a village massacre. "You are not allowed on Facebook, Charlie Cooper. That is the rule. No Facebook until you're eighteen!"

"It's Instagram, Mom." I try to inform. "A place where a community of people post their favorite family pictures."

She's kinda slobbering at this point. "I hate, hate, hate Facebook. And the little creep who started it. I hate him, too." She tries to shut the computer.

"But Mom," I say as reasonably as I know how, "social media is the news of our generation." I look into her eyes and wonder, When will old people get that? I also wonder how she thinks she can stop me when I know my way around a computer the way she knows her way around a newspaper.

"There will be no generation if you flunk out of school." She points to the door. "Good luck, baby!"

On our way to school, I'm not even thinking about all the people who hate me. It's almost like that part of my life is over. I've moved on. All I can think about is the audition. The lines. The character named Josie that is so ME. She's cute and sassy and just the right amount of mean. And then, after I'm done thinking about that, I think about not having to go to school anymore. A tutor on set? Is there any more magical sentence than that? Soon, very soon, none of these people will matter anymore. Not Lillian, or Erica, not Marta or Pickler. Not even Bobby. I'm in my own little Nirvana when Pen's loud scratchy voice cuts in.

"Wait up!" Pen catches up with me.

I stop. "What?"

"Mom told me you want to cancel the Halloween party."

"Yeah, well . . ." I'm expecting her to argue, to actually dig and dig until she finds the real reason I don't want the party.

But instead she looks relieved. "Thanks. I hated the idea all along."

"You did?"

"How can we throw a party when animals are being killed by greed and bulldozers?" She points to the entrance of Stanley Hill where the megamansions are being built. There's dirt and water streaming down the hill. "Just look at that." She points to the river of sludge.

"Horrible." I toss my water bottle in an open trash can.

Pen runs to reclaim it. She reaches in, finds it, and turns. "Blue, Charlie, how many times have I got to tell you?"

"I'm sorry." And I am. I swear.

"The canyons are dying," she says sadly.

"Can we go now?" Felix pushes us from behind. We pass the water house on the right. An entire house built over the hot springs. Next to it, there's a vacant lot of boulders and grassy hills. Legend is, the Houdini tunnels go under the street and come through that lot. Just looking at it makes me want to start digging. I walk faster. I can't wait for this day to end.

One Step at a Time

I walk into the classroom to find Bobby, who looks up from his death drawings to glare at me.

I look down, start rummaging through my backpack, then say softly, "I'm sorry your dad's having problems—" But before I can finish, he loses it.

"My dad!" he practically spits at me. "What do you know about my dad?"

"Uh," I stammer, "the drugs, the career—"

"My dad"—he looks like he wants to punch me—"has nothing to do with this. You lied to me. You're always lying, Cooper. That's what you do—you lie."

"I just wanted to say I'm sorry, all right?"

He totally ignores me.

TRUE FACT: Forget the marriage. Our friendship is broken.

"Ladies and gentlemen, quiet down." Mr. L sees what's going on. I look around and notice Marta's still not here. "This weekend is Halloween, and with Halloween comes—"

"Cavities!" Marjorie squeals. I've heard that Marjorie's parents give out a pack of toothpaste, toothbrush, and floss on Halloween.

I look over to see if Bobby rolls his eyes like he normally would. But he's gone, his hood pulled up, just a profile.

"The one day of the year when the spirits emerge from the underworld and meet us in ours. It is a time when we can walk with them and talk to them."

"I don't believe in them," I state plainly.

"Which is a good thing," Erica points out. "God knows there's enough live people who hate your guts." Everyone laughs.

Ha, ha. "Keep laughing." Soon I'll be schooled on the set with all the other big-time celebs and I'll never have to listen to their little voices again.

"You think you're gonna be a big shot?" Lillian fills the silence. "Don't need any of us, is that right, Cooper?"

She doesn't know how right she is. I look up at the clock. One hour and fifteen minutes. That's all I have left of my miserable life.

When the snack bell rings, I get up and stretch. "Time to

go," I announce to the back row. "My limo is waiting."

They laugh like I'm a liar.

Bobby grabs his ball and starts bouncing. His friends gather around. "Yo, Cooper, where do you think you're going?"

Thank God they ask, because I so want everyone to know. "Hollywood," I say. "And I'm never looking back."

"Limo, huh?" Lillian grins like she knows something. "Can I see?"

"I thought you'd never ask." I grab my backpack. "See ya, Mr. L. Thanks for everything."

"Sure, Charlie," he says, clueless that this just might be the last time he sees me.

Erica gets to the door before me, an unusual smile on her lips. "No hard feelings?"

"None at all." I blow into her face. I hope my breath stinks. "I have to go. Car's waiting." She steps aside. I can feel their eyes on my back. I can feel their jealousy, and I have to say I love every minute of it. Bobby's bouncing the ball. "Hey, Bobby." I give him one last try. "You want to come see?"

"Limos are not my style." He shakes his head and walks away, like he couldn't care less if he ever sees me again.

That's the last time I beg. I pull my shoulders back and I focus on all the good that's about to come my way. Why? Because I worked for it. "My limo awaits," I call out to the world. "Look out, Hollywood, I'm coming!" I walk across the upper yard, slowly, hoping to gather as many people as I can. I want their last memory of me, Charlie C. Cooper, to be getting into a limo. I turn around. The crowd is huge. I pull open the door leading to the parking lot. One look at my black, shiny, major-swag limo with the TLC in white cursive and the dude in the black suit and cap, and they'll forget every bad thing they've ever heard. They rush to the door.

The parking lot's a boring sea of eco-conscious Priuses.

Babs giggles. "Where's the limo, Charlie?"

My face gets hot. I'm sure it's red. "He's probably grabbing Selena Gomez on the way," I announce fearlessly. I look around the lot, and lean back against the wall.

Five minutes later, a broken-down junkyard car pulls into the lot. Dark-gray smoke is shooting out of its dragging exhaust pipe. The driver looks right at me and hits his fist against the horn. *Beep! Beep!* He waves.

I gasp. No! No! It can't be for me.

The driver gets out. His belly is falling out from under his dirty brownish-white tank top. Tank top! He's covered in dark curly hair. "Anyone know a kid called Charlie?" He looks down at a crumpled-up sheet of paper. "Charlie Cooper?"

I turn away. It can't be.

Lillian has the look of sweet victory. "Charlie"—she points right at me—"your limo awaits."

The crowd laughs. Erica yells out, "Hey, everyone, come and check out Charlie's limo."

"It's a mistake." It has to be a mistake. He loved the head

shots. He said I was going to be a huge star.

"No, Charlie." Erica pulls out her cell phone and snaps away. "It's exactly what you deserve."

I walk toward the car. Everyone is huddled in the doorway, watching, waiting for that moment when they can see me in the car.

His accent is thick and bored. "Get in. I still have to get lunch." He falls into the driver's seat and doesn't even lift a finger to help me. I get in. They laugh. But I don't give them the satisfaction of looking back. From this moment on, I only look forward. I'm going to have it written into my contract that I will never accept a ride from this man again.

The door handle is covered with sticky grease. The seat is plastic and ripped. He guns the engine; thick pollution shoots from the car. The kindergartners and first graders run to the back fence and look out.

"There's my sister Charlie!" Felix screams through the chain link fence. "Where's she going?"

I duck as low as I can.

"Jail, I hope," answers a little girl. "They say she's super mean."

What a little brat, right? I close my eyes to avoid looking into anyone else's as we drive into Beverly Hills. I'm almost home.

Moment of Truth

He drops me in front of the Holy Grail, the William Morris Endeavor offices on Wilshire in Beverly Hills. Put it this way: if I had to die, I'd do it right now, in front of all those mirrors reflecting nothing but the heavens above. I stand before the sleek double doors, like Dorothy before Oz, and am humbled. Not even the flowers dare to droop. All buds are exactly aligned, damp, and ready to open. Perfection. This is how I want my world to look. I push open the door, and the moment my foot crosses the threshold, I catch someone jumping out of the bushes to wipe off my fingerprints. Efficiency, thy name is Hollywood.

I feel like I'm in the engine room of the great movie-making machine. It's cold and quiet, too, which is strange, because it's full of people talking and walking fast from one place to the next like there isn't a second to lose. I feel the intense electricity, and man, oh, man, do I like it. At school all we do is waste time. It's a goal—like, let's see how fast we can make the day go. But here, every second counts. I dig that.

"Charlie." Chad's suddenly in front of me. He puts out his hand to shake mine. He's all business. "Great to see you. I'll have my assistant call your parents to let them know you're here."

I follow him down a curved white hallway and into a large, cold conference room. I stop and stare. Boy, oh, boy, does this place look like a funeral home or what? It's as cold as a freezer. There's a massive flat screen on the wall that glows against the white wall. The table is long and oval, and there are six super-old and grumpy-looking people sitting there. They look like they've never cracked a smile. Please tell me that these are not the people I am basing all my hopes and dreams on.

Chad pushes me forward. "Charlie, meet the team behind the show *Off the Beam*."

Suddenly I feel like everything is riding on this moment.

Slow my heart.

Slow my heart.

Slow my heart.

They lean forward. Their chairs squeak. Their pencils are armed and ready to take notes. To examine me. "Hello, Charlie."

I gulp and wave. My heart is beating so fast, I'm more scared and nervous than I have ever been. I pull my pair of lucky black lens-free glasses out of my pocket and pop 'em on my nose. I mush up my hair and fix the pink sequin skull-and-crossbones barrette. And then, my peeps, I go for it. I am on.

"Hello, Hollywood." I look at each and every one of them. Their eyes are on me like they're eating me up. They jot down notes, whisper, write a little more. "The name's Charlie C. Cooper, and I am a middle child." For the first time in my life I announce it with pride. "I can act, sing, and I'm"—I take a deep breath—"great at gymnastics."

They smile and take notes. They look pretty pleased.

"Exactly how long have you been doing gymnastics, Charlie?" Chad asks.

"I started when I was one," I say with complete confidence.

"One?" He gives me a weird look.

"Hi, Charlie, my name is Bernice." Her face folds into a thousand wrinkles. "I'm the creator of the series."

"Hi, Bernice." I maintain eye contact and wave sweetly. Grown-ups love that.

"Now, on a scale of one to ten"—Bernice gets her pencil ready—"how much do you value friendship?"

I know what this is about. And I am ready for it. "Ten. All the way, ten."

"And the truth?"

Say what? Is it hot in here?

124

"The truth, Charlie," she repeats.

"Ten." I blurt out. "Can't have friends without it, right?"

"Now, Charlie, we normally don't take kids who have zero acting experience." She leans back, lets her glasses fall to her big chest. She's got them on those librarian ropes. "But you caught our attention. You know why?"

I play with my glasses. "Because of what happened at school?"

She nods. "Frankly, we need a new hero. The kind of hero troubled kids can relate to. A flawed hero."

"Well, if you want flawed, look no further," I say to each and every one of them. "As a middle child, I've overcome a lot." I put both hands on the desk and lean over. "Let me tell you, it's not easy being me."

"Well, then let's see what you can do with being Josie." Chad points to a wall. He hits a button, and the curtains pull back to reveal a solid glass wall. Inside the room there is a beam and mats.

"It's soundproof." He winks. "We can hear them, but they can't hear us. Unless I touch this button."

I think I'm in love. "May I?" I go to play with the button when the boring old suit interrupts my fun.

He gets in my face like I'm a little kid. "You know why it's called *Off the Beam*?"

"Yeah, because my character is always trying to push someone off the beam to get on the team, and she'll use any way she can to do it." I grin. Just thinking about it makes me happy.

"That's correct," the lady says. "And you're aware of the whole point of the show?"

Uh, hello! Of course I know. "That she gets *on* the beam!" I laugh. "I'm so perfect for this part, you will die when you see me. I was born to play Josie."

The old man begins again. He's got zero fashion sense and even less hair. Not to be rude or anything. "The girl you'd be playing—"

Yes! The girl I would be playing sounds like it's a go. This is going so well, I can hardly stand it.

"She would learn that she can't get on the team by her underhandedness. That is her character arc. She learns to do things the honest way. That's what we want kids to take from this." The lady pauses to make sure I get it. I get it, all right.

But to be perfectly honest (which of course I can't be), I think that whole thing is dumb.

"Do you understand, Charlie?" the woman asks *again*.

"Yes, ma'am." Of course I'm not going to tell her she's wrong. That she has no clue about her audience. What kid wants a lesson in their show, huh? "Should I show you my routine?" I get up and do a few stretches. "It's pretty impressive."

But Chad tells me to sit. "There's another person auditioning for the part. You're next."

Whoa, hold on a second. What did he say? I whisper to him, "I thought you said I was their top choice?"

The lights dim, and we watch the room. I try to calm my nerves by repeating to myself: No way can anyone be as good as me. I go through the reasons:

- I'm funny.
- I'm original.
- I've spent my whole life trying to get what I want by any means available.
- I've got a trendsetting fashion sense.

But then the door to the soundproof room opens. A girl walks in. My stomach drops. It's Marta.

Can you believe it? Marta. That's it. God hates me, hates me. She's wearing her signature floppy leotard from 1972, and her hair is stuck up in a high beehive. I'm pretty sure she's got egg stains on her front. They all lean forward and blink. A lot. Like they can't believe what they're looking at.

They slap the table. "She's perfect!"

"So real!"

"So relatable."

"Vulnerable yet powerful. I love it."

"Hello, Marta." Chad speaks into the intercom. "We're all here. Please begin."

She nods confidently before hopping up onto the beam. And the second she does, you can tell she'll be an Olympic athlete one day. I want to look away. Better yet, I want to run away. But I can't. Even I want to watch her. Marta completes a perfect routine on the beam. It's downright disgusting. Her arms and legs are so powerful, so light, she floats through the air like she's flying. And when she lands, I can hear the sharp inhale. They cover their faces like they can't believe what they just saw. I want to puke.

Chad hits the button. "Beautiful. Just gorgeous. Thank you, Marta Urloff." Chad turns to me.

"Amazing, isn't she? Incredible?"

"And you knew it all along." He shakes his head at me. "You knew, and you lied. I'm not interested in lying clients."

"I don't see it as lying, but as protecting—" I look at all their faces.

"Nice," Chad grins.

"I'm not kidding—she and her guardian are totally committed to her future as an Olympian. You said this would take total commitment, remember?"

"You also lied about yourself."

I slam my hand against the table. "Now that's going too far."

"Really?" Chad opens his laptop and quickly types something. A video appears. He taps play. I can hear my voice. Marta's voice is next. I know exactly what this is and why he's playing it.

"Where did you get this?" I ask, but I already know. Greta.

"You had no idea how to do anything on the beam at all.

You got Marta to train you." Long pause. "In fact," he continues hammering me, "you lied to me about every single thing."

TRUE FACT: Whenever you're caught in a huge lie, break it into little pieces.

I work the room, turning on my charm. "I did it because I know I am the best person for the job. Hands down." I look into each and every set of eyes. "I really studied the script. The part of Josie doesn't even hang on gymnastics, does it?" I walk around the table. "It hangs on personality. Believability. Am I right, people?"

They nod. Chad nods.

I can feel it. They're coming over to my side. "Marta. She's great at gymnastics. Yes. But she's an only child. She's never had to be underhanded. See what I'm saying?" I can see they're listening. "And between you and me, she's got zero sense of humor. That's why she isn't right for this. Trust me, I know."

The suits turn. "She was very funny on that video."

"Because she was with me. Don't you see?" I shout out. "I'm the funny one. Trust me, she is so not funny."

"I laugh just looking at her," says one old guy.

"But not in a *good* way." I'm fighting for my life here. "And you need total commitment. She has no time. Zero. And then there's her aunt with the mole, who doesn't speak English—"

"Stop. Get out here before you make it any worse." Chad opens the door and points to the audition room.

"But I can't beat that." I look at him.

"Oh, I know. I represent her too now, so either way I win."

"Great." I walk out into the hallway. Marta's aunt is standing outside, wearing her Romanian red-and-white tracksuit and doing some weird gypsy voodoo hand signals at my face. I avoid looking at her for fear I will have nightmares of being attacked by her giant hairy mole.

Greta spits on the floor. "You are thief."

Marta is standing right by the door I'm supposed to go through. I stop in front of her. "I know you hate me, but you're being played. Watch out." And then I slip into the audition room. The room is cold and silent. I can't see the suits and Chad looking at me from the other side. I strip down to my supersparkly leotard. The intercom buzzes.

"Begin," Chad says. Is it my imagination, or is he being meaner to me than he was to Marta?

I look at the beam, massage it, try and make it my friend. I'll never beat Marta on skill. So I'll have to beat her on personality.

"Any time now." Chad taps.

I put my hands on the beam, take a deep breath, and lift myself up and over into a straddle. I can feel my heart through my leotard. Keep your cool, Charlie, I tell myself. I lift my leg and stand. You're halfway there.

Chad beeps in. "Come on, we don't have all day now."

I stand tall and stretch high. Focus, Charlie, focus. Don't even think about them. I reach my hands up and find a spot I can focus on. I do a split leap as high as I can and I land on the beam. I can't believe it! I'm killing it! I turn, do a little hand thing that looks kinda cool, and make another leap. And then when I'm coming down, my foot slips, my other leg scrapes the side of the beam and I fall flat on my face.

I slap the mat. "And it was all going so well!" I yell into the room.

The intercom clicks. "Uh, not really."

"Thanks, Chad. Thanks a lot."

"Get up, finish it," he says.

I push away all thoughts of Marta smiling and get back up on that cruel beam. I raise my hands high, flick my wrists, and do my best gymnast face—like I just had a huge whiff of tuna. Split leaps. I start to run and do the little splits in the air. I'm smiling, get ready to plant my hands for a final cartwheel off the end, when—*bam!*

My hand loses its grip and I fall like a giant lump of goo on my side. That's it. I'm done. I don't even try to get up. I pound the mat and cry. I even forget anyone's there until I hear the click of the intercom.

"You done?" Chad's coldhearted voice comes in loud and clear.

"Done. Yeah. I'm done." I sit up and stare at the beam. How can one piece of wood be so complicated? "I can never beat her, can't you understand? That's why I didn't want her to come!" I yell at them. I scoop up my clothes and leave the room. Marta is still standing in the hall right where I left her.

Marta laughs at me. "Looks like *you're* the one who got played. And you lost."

"It's yours. Have it all." I storm out, past her nasty aunt and her hairy mole. I'm done.

Chad and the suits walk out of their room. "Charlie, where do you think you're going?"

I march right past him, down the hallway, wearing my leotard and ripped tights, and Converse in hand. "I quit." I hit the elevator button as many times as I can. "Open!"

The elevator opens and closes, with me in it.

The End

Well, that's it, people. You may as well stop reading now. It's all downhill from here, from *not* being hired by ABC Family to getting dumped by Chad at dumb old WME to being forced into the car from hell to being stared at by eco-freaks as we chug up Laurel Canyon in a broken-down car full of toxic fumes—and I'm not talking about the guy's wet armpit hair.

Chad, the Hollywood hypocrite. Marta and her money-grubbing aunt. Wasn't one shot at the American dream enough? They had to steal mine? I hated them all. In fact, the list of people I hated was way longer than the list of people I didn't.

"Drop me here," I tell the guy when we get to the top of my driveway. He doesn't argue this time. See, even he thinks I'm a has-been. My legs are stuck to the seat, but I peel them off and crawl out the back door, my clothes in my hands, my hair a wreck. He turns the car around and doesn't look back.

That's the last of it, the end of my hopes and dreams. There's nothing left for me to do except go and talk to Mr. Houdini himself. I often feel like he hears me, like he understands. I climb on the wall to sit with him. I know he knows what this feels like. I can see it in his eyes. But see, here's the difference: he was the kind of guy who could get back up no matter what. Not me.

I'm starving and depressed. Food—food would make me feel better. I make my way along the wall. I tiptoe up to the front of the house and peek in. No one is in the kitchen. Mom and Dad had appointments today. So the coast is clear. I open the fridge to find a brand-new piece of Brie and a new container of tapenade, and I pull the fresh baguette right out of its bakery sleeve. I slip all of it in my shirt, grab a bottle of Pellegrino, and run up the stairs, back to my room. My soul needs healing.

I call Jai. He's my soul man. My one and only friend. "Hey, Jai." I cut a huge slab of Brie and stick it on a piece of bread.

"Hello, my American friend." He picks up the laptop and moves through the slum.

I see a whole lot of people cleaning floors, pushing trash, washing sidewalks. "Hey, what's going on?"

"Very big news. *60 Minutes*, a very famous American TV news show, is coming to film a wealthy Indian who has built the largest house in the world."

I fix my pillows, settle into my bed, and take another wonderful bite. Being home alone is just what the doctor ordered. "So what's that have to do with the slums?"

"The house is built in the middle of the slums. Like a giant penthouse shooting straight up sixty floors." He smiles. "The billionaire has hired untouchables to clean all his waste. The Americans are very interested in this."

Untouchable? I stop eating. "What's an untouchable?"

"Ah." Jai shakes his head like there are so many bad things. "In India, it is said to be the lowest form of humanity. These are the people who clean toilets, cremate the dead, remove dead animals from the road, and cut the cords of babies when they are born. They look the same as me, but they are different. Everyone knows who they are, and they are avoided like the Black Death."

I repeat in my mind: *Everyone knows who they are, and they are avoided like the Black Death.*

That's it. I, Charlie Cooper, am an untouchable. "So how do they stop being an untouchable?"

"They accept their fate, just as we all must." Jai looks behind his back.

I shove the last bit of Brie into my mouth and wash it down with some Pellegrino. "But how can you do that when your fate sucks?"

He gets up again and walks. The slums have great wireless. "I'm sorry, Charlie, but I must make myself scarce before the television cameras come. There's still the matter of the Russian mob hunting me down."

"Fine, just go," I say angrily. Guess he doesn't want to talk to an untouchable either. I curl into a ball and search through Google images for the best untouchable outfit ever.

And then I guess I passed out.

Toss This in the Trash:
I Am No Role Model

I wake up to Pen yelling at the top of her lungs, "Charlie!"

Next I feel her hands on me, shaking me in a not-so-nice way. "Wake up!"

I'm totally dazed, still half dreaming. It was all so clear. I was in India, dressed in tons of silk robes, covered in jewels and cremating Lillian on a massive funeral pyre, over the great Ganges River, and I was surprisingly at peace.

"Charlie, you have to see this." Pen grabs her computer, types something into Google. Up pops my audition, which of course was videotaped and leaked by Marta's ungrateful aunt. "It's gone viral."

I read the numbers on the bottom of the video. Eighty thousand views. It's only been three hours. What the heck?

TRUE FACT: We love to watch our heroes crash and burn.

I fall back on my bed of crumbs and Brie. "Is there no dignity left?"

"Soon you'll have more views than Psy." Pen plays the video of my total breakdown, analyzing every move. "What the heck happened?"

My eyes fell on the paused image of me lying on the beam. "I was ambushed."

"So Lillian sent Marta over there?" Pen replays it for the third time.

I watch as I fall and cry, fall and cry, over and over again. They fast-forwarded it and then rewound it so it looks like I just keep falling and crying. They've put on the sound of a baby crying at a high pitch, also playing it backward and forward. Nice touch.

"So what does Lillian get?" Pen looks at me. "That's the question."

She hits play on the YouTube video *again*. I slap the computer shut. "How about my total humiliation?"

The door swings open. Dad pokes his head in. "Charlie?"

I plaster a fake smile on. "Hey, Dad."

Dad doesn't know. "So, so, how'd it go today, Charlie? Tell me everything."

Felix screams from downstairs, "No one gets the computer!!!" even though no one is near the computer.

Mom comes running into our room. "Hey, baby, did you get it?"

I wish I could hide under my blanket.

"Charlie?" Mom's voice is suddenly sad. "Are you okay?"

I take a deep breath. "Well——"

"Marta got it." Pen cuts me off.

"Marta?" Mom looks all perplexed. "I thought she didn't want it."

"She changed her mind" is all I want to say on the subject.

Mom nods like it's no big deal when it's the biggest deal of my entire life. "We should have them over to celebrate, make up for the lie you told——"

"Mom!" I cut her off. Dad stares at me with that horrible look that basically says *I know what you've done*. I haven't had the time to tell Dad yet. And I want to be the one to tell him. I don't want him to think I'm a liar, because if there's one thing Dad can't stand, it's a liar. Pen turns her back to us and opens a book. She pretends to read, but the tension in the room is louder than any noise could ever be.

Mom takes one look at me and says, "Well, tell him yourself."

Suddenly it's so quiet. Dad looks at us and smiles like the last one in on a secret.

"Tell me what?"

And me, I start to sweat. I just can't take one more person hating me right now. I'm not going to lie, it's been pretty rough. I have no one.

"Well?" Dad's waiting.

"Um." I'm thinking of a way to put it.

I'm struggling, when all of a sudden Pen cuts in. "Yeah, so maybe Charlie kept the audition quiet." Pen gets up and points right at me like she's my lawyer. "But you know what Charlie did in return?"

Dad looks right at me.

"Charlie"—Pen gets between us—"got Marta into the JOs. Got Pickler to pay for her flight and her registration."

I am warm with gratitude.

"That's nice." Dad plays with a string dangling from his shorts. "But . . ." He rips the thread and pushes Pen's chair so there's nothing between him and me. "It doesn't change the fact that you were underhanded."

"Underhanded. My middle name."

"Stop," Dad says, all mad. "That's not you and you know it." And then he smiles. "You're better now. Much better, Charlie."

I'm not so sure.

He comes over to me and squeezes my shoulder. "Marta won. You need to be a good sport about it, because you deserve what you got."

"It's karma." Mom drops it like a flower.

I wanted to stick karma right up her—

"I also think we need to move on." Dad gets up and claps. "What do you say we have that Halloween party after all?" Dad says like it's going to erase my loss.

I roll my eyes.

"The place looks great. We could do it to raise money for the wildlife corridor—how's that, Pen?"

Pen thinks about it for a while, mulls it over. "You know, that's a fine idea, Dad."

Traitor. I glare at her.

"And Charlie, you could invite all your friends," he says.

"I told you. I have *no* friends, and I'm not just saying that. I mean I have *zero* friends." It's really quite an accomplishment to go from being on the news, about to have a hit TV show and possibly even a hot boyfriend, to zero. All in one week.

"Oh, come on. Of course you have friends." Dad rubs my shoulders.

TRUE FACT: Parents never believe you when you say you have *no* friends.

"Marta will forgive you," Mom says. "Call her at home. Talk to her. Talk to Greta. After all you've done for them, how can they not?"

I shake my head in despair. Do grown-ups ever learn? Do they ever listen?

And at school, forget it. They've tasted blood. My blood.

They've turned into a pack of wolves. When I pass, they huddle and laugh. Or stick out a foot and trip me. There's no way around them. Even Bobby thinks whatever comes out of my mouth is a lie.

She rubs my shoulders. "You can always talk to Dr. Scales."

Dr. Scales? The last thing I want is to go backward. Plus, what can he do for me? Nothing. I look down and focus all my energy on trying to calm my exploding heart. This, by the way, is a technique I'd read about from Mandela. He said that when the dogs were put on him, he would close his eyes and still his heart. So that's what I do.

Life Stinks
and Then You Die

I decide to take a walk. It's after school gets out, so the coast should be way clear. Just in case, I put on my trusty black-frame glasses and pull on one of Mom's huge scary garden hats. That way, even if anyone recognizes me, they'll pretend they don't. I pass by the old log house on the corner that sits on stilts over the hot springs. Next to it is the open field with those huge boulders, rock walls, and green moss. The fence is locked. There's no car in the garage. No trespassing signs are all over the place. I stop and stare. I peek over the fence. And then I jump.

And land in another world.

I stand on a ledge, surrounded by water. Not the clear blue water of swimming pools, but the thick green water of underground springs. Koi fish jump to greet me. I walk along the

143

railing and go around the side of the house where I can see the field. Somewhere, hidden in the rocks and hills and the thick grass, or maybe tucked into the abandoned chimney, is another door to the Houdini tunnels. I'd bet my life on it. Not that it's worth much anymore.

I walk down to the bottom of the property, past the pool and the Jacuzzi covered with leaves, and stand at the fence, which lines busy Laurel Canyon Boulevard. I peek through the slats and see our house across the way. I wish I could hide here forever.

Suddenly a car pulls over and blocks my view. The door opens. It's Bobby. He practically jumps out of a shiny new car and slams the door. His dad's still talking, but Bobby's not listening. He's walking with his head down, like he just wants to be left alone. I catch a glimpse of them. His dad has his hand on the lady's knee, and she has her hand on top of his. She's giggling like life's a ball. Lucky them—at least someone's happy. I watch them drive off, thinking how great it would be to be old—not the veiny wrinkle part, but the driver's license part—when suddenly a rock goes whizzing past me.

"Yo! You're trespassing."

I turn around, and there's Bobby.

I'm so impressed by his ninja-like entry that I totally forget how much he hates me, how he dropped me like a rotten piece of stinky cheese when the whole school was chanting "Scorpion."

He shifts the backpack. The contents clink. "What are you doing here?"

"Trying to get away." I wonder what he's got in there. More paint?

His eyes are red and mad. He's not letting me in. "Can you go now, please?"

"Why? You own it?" I'm sick and tired of everyone out there thinking they have more of a right to be mad than I do.

"Get off my back." Bobby pulls his hoodie over his head, grabs his skateboard, and climbs the old rock steps that look like they've been here since the Native Americans. Sharp oak leaves crunch under his sneakers.

And I thought I was in a bad mood. "What's up with you, Bobby Brown?" I chase after him. The rock trail is steep and covered with leaves, trash, and weird objects like stuffed animals and Mexican candles. "I get that your dad has some trouble."

Bobby stomps his feet and gives me one of his famous glares.

"But do you really want to enter a whose-life-sucks-more competition?" I'm so out of breath that I stop halfway. "Because I will so beat you." The words echo through the rocks and still sound empty. "*Your* life compared to mine is like a trip to Six Flags." Still, he doesn't respond. I keep going. "Your parents are giggling, you made it onto the basketball team, and everyone loves you. I mean, seriously! Do you know how lucky you are compared to me?"

Bobby bends down to examine something in the leaves. He's totally ignoring me, of course, like I am making no sense. But the fact is, he should be paying me for my words of wisdom. After all, I have been under psychiatric care. I have insight.

He walks off up the hill, crossing paths like he's been here a thousand times. I wonder if there are snakes. There have to be snakes.

"From where I stand," I add, "you have no reason to act like such a jerk to me."

Bobby whips around and comes running down the path straight at me. He's snorting, he's so mad. "For your information, that 'lady' in the car"—his eyes are tormented, his hands are in my face—"is *not* my mom, so quit telling me how lucky I am. Damn it." He turns and runs back up the hill.

"Your aunt?"

"No." His loose caramel-colored afro is so blond at the tips it looks like he dyed it. Lucky. I wish my hair bounced when I walked.

I catch up to him just as he jumps into one of the rock caves that line the mountain. He looks at me like I'm an intruder. "It's his new girlfriend, all right?"

"Your mom is letting your dad have a girlfriend?" I lift off my hat. "That's what I call progressive."

"No, dumb butt." He drops his bag. It makes a huge clang. "Just found out my dad left me and my mom for the new girlfriend. All this time they've been lying to me, saying everything was fine, couples fight, blah, blah, blah. Liars." He cocks his head. "Just like you."

So I'm mixed in there too. In that big bag of misery. "I'm sorry, Bobby. I didn't know."

"Yeah, well." Suddenly he doesn't sound like he wants to kill me anymore. "Don't worry about me. I'll figure it out." He puts out his hand and pulls me into the cave.

I look around and can't believe it. There are gems glued to the rock walls, and they twinkle like stars. There are drawings, books, magazines too. In the corner is a sleeping bag and pillow. "Is this all yours?"

He nods.

It feels like a mountain retreat, a place to be totally away from it all. "I love it."

"Me too." He looks around, proud and slightly in awe of the place that no one knows about but him.

And then I realize that we're holding hands, which feels pretty great and pretty awkward, because hours ago he wanted to slice my head off.

"You know your sad audition is all over YouTube?" He drops my hand, picks up a leaf, and smells it. "Life is pretty much gonna suck for you from now on."

I think about Jai's description of the untouchables. "I've accepted my fate, Bobby." I look out over the hills and the street. "Everything I touch turns to poo. So I'm not gonna touch anything anymore. I am going to be an untouchable."

"And what's that, Cooper?" Bobby's laughing at me already.

"Someone who can't be touched. My friend in India told me all about them." Funny how things have changed. Up until a few weeks ago, I was going for Mother Teresa and Gandhi, and now I'm at the other end of the line. The person who can't be touched. Me. In the end, it's easier.

Bobby elbows me. "Ah, come on. You're tougher than that."

I shake my head. "I'm not. I don't have it in me anymore, Bobby. Because whatever I do, it always comes back to bite me on the butt."

But Bobby's not feeling all that sympathetic. "You threw Marta under the bus. You lied to her, to me, to everyone—"

I can feel myself getting riled up. I'm about to launch into it again when I stop myself. I just stop arguing. It doesn't matter anymore.

"All of it just to get some dumb TV show." He keeps going, needing to have his say. "What did you expect? People to love you?"

TRUE FACT: Sometimes people can't handle the truth.

We lean back against the cool walls with a clear view of my house on the other side. Both of us silent, lost in our own troubles. When the silence gets too much for me, I ask, "You know who owns this place?"

148

"Tarzan." Bobby picks up a stick and writes his name in the dirt. "He was so famous back in the old days. Now he's all alone and walks around naked most of the time. Doesn't leave the house much. I've been coming through here for years, to get to the caves. He's cool as long as you don't mess with his house." He drops the stick and rubs his eyes.

I crawl out and look around. "Legend is there's a tunnel entrance on this side." The back of the mountain is laced with rock caves, caves big enough for a lion to rest in. "I can feel it in my bones."

"That's right—you're the tunnel hunter." Bobby smiles like a kid again. "Mr. L's sure there's gold in the caves here too. Something about a Mexican bandit who hid his treasure when the Americans took California."

Bobby watches the men working on our house across the way. "I want to find it. And then I want to run away. Wanna run with me?"

I'm melting. Words can't form in my brain. I see the two of us on the run. Holding hands. Sharing Hostess fruit pies. Blueberry.

Then it's over. He jumps from the cave. The bag moves. Sounds like glass.

I eye the bag. "What's in there?"

"Something that feels good." He jumps.

I follow him down the rock steps that crisscross the hill. When we get to the property line on the far left, he points to a boulder with a red target chalked on it. "See that?"

"Yep."

"Pretend it's, oh, I don't know. Lillian." He takes a shiny glass bottle from his bag and hurls it at the target. Glass shatters. He turns to see my face, my reaction.

"Or my dad's new girlfriend." He takes another and another, hurling each one with more force than the last. His face gets redder and redder, his screams get louder and louder with each shatter. Finally he turns, wipes his forehead, and asks me, "You wanna try?"

"Breaking bottles? Really?" How childish. How like a boy. "How pointless."

He comes toward me, holding a bottle, with a grin on his face that can't be good. "Just try. Just once."

I reach out and take the clear glass Coke bottle by the neck.

"Okay. Stand here." He draws a line in the packed leaves. "Now, take it over your shoulders, hold the top of the bottle, and flick it like hell." He watches me lift it. "Like that, that's right."

I pull back my arm, bend my knees, and throw it with all my might. It lands with a thud—straight into the leaves. Quite frankly I am shocked. I have a good arm. "What happened?"

Bobby cracks up. "You really suck." He gets the bottle and puts it in my hand and shows me how to hurl it.

"All right, I got it." I push him away. "This is gonna be a bull's-eye." And I throw the bottle with all my might. I hit the target, but again the bottle lands with a thud.

He laughs. "Man, Cooper, you're seriously hopeless. I had no idea you were such a girl."

A girl? Did he really just say that?

Suddenly all I can think about is getting that unbreakable bottle and smashing it to smithereens. "A girl, huh?" I run and grab the bottle. The skin of my finger snags on a crack. Blood lifts from the cut and dribbles down my hand like chocolate syrup. "Dang it!" I drop the bottle.

"Hey, Coop? You okay?" Bobby rips a piece of his shirt and comes down to wrap it around my bleeding finger. "Does it hurt?"

I wait for the pain to start, for the gash to throb, but you know what? It's not half as bad as all the stuff I've been going through at school.

Bobby's warm chocolate eyes and caterpillar lashes are locked on mine. "I'm . . ." He pauses, trips over his words, looks away.

"What?"

"Nothing."

I push him. "What nothing?"

He shrugs, slouching his shoulders. "Sorry, all right?"

I bend my finger. I didn't want to think about it anymore.

Bobby digs his hands into his pockets. "I should have stuck around, stood by you."

"Yeah, well, whatever." I don't want to go backward. Plus, my finger throbs.

"If you stop lying to me, I promise not to run." He puts his hand out. "Deal?"

Really? Will he? I don't know, but I shake it anyway.

Bobby grins like the good old days. He hands me another bottle. "Try again."

"Okay." I take it, cock it back behind my head, and take aim.

I see Lillian.

I see Chad.

I see Erica.

I see Marta.

I see me.

It shatters against the target. "Yes!" I jump in the air. Bobby gives me a high five on my noninjured hand. He hands me another. He's right. With each shattering explosion of glass, I feel better.

When there were no more bottles and the sun was gone, Bobby and I crawled back over the fence into the real world.

Bobby stops halfway over the fence. "You still doing Halloween at your place?"

"Me?" I pull a branch out of my hair. "No." I laugh. "I'm hiding. In my room. Until day breaks. That's my Halloween."

Bobby nods like he gets it. "Just hang tight, Coop." He drops his board. He looks so hot I can barely stand it. "All this will blow over."

How? I wonder.

"It's gonna be good—you'll see." And he skates away, all happy and relaxed. I wish I felt the same. I glance down at my finger. The blood has turned a dark brown. If only everything healed this fast.

My Metaphorical Stoning

By five o'clock on Halloween, the place looks like the scariest set of a horror movie you've ever seen. Spiders and rats hang from the trees. Felix has thrown toilet paper all over our house, then sprayed it with red "blood." Jumbo black crows squawk from every tree. Fog spews out from one of the fifty or so fog machines they've hidden all over the property. Red guts are pouring out of dead rats and crows made of fake fur. The tunnel door is wide-open, the dirt about one-quarter of the way removed. Mom put a skeleton in it, making it look like he was climbing out.

If I wasn't so depressed, I'd invite the world and tell them I did it all. Pen's been working on her costume all day long, sitting over the sewing machine. She's going as a dead Laurel Canyon squirrel, so she put on a squirrel's tail and poured fake blood all over herself. She took a family poll, and no one knew what she was, so she wrote SAVE THE CANYON'S SQUIRRELS on her T-shirt.

Whatever.

And Felix, the poor kid, is getting totally used by Mom and Dad. They're making him wear this huge bunny costume. "I look so dumb," he says as he tries to sit on his bed but falls onto the floor.

"Kids, kids! Are you ready? Come on, it's Halloween!" Mom runs into our room. Her boobs are totally hanging out.

Pen's horrified. "You should really cover those up."

I personally think she looks decades younger. "You look awesome."

"And you, what's your costume?" Mom walks around me, studies my pj's. "Depressed teen?"

I throw her a high five.

"Baby, it can't be that bad." Mom sits next to me, rubs my arm. "You still have friends."

"She really doesn't, Mom," Pen cuts in. "Marta's joined forces with the populars. There's no one left."

Mom holds out a black mask. "Here—no one will know it's you."

Mask and pj's—my costume this year. "Thanks, but no thanks."

Pen can't take her eyes off Mom's costume. "Moms shouldn't show their boobs unless they're feeding someone."

"I'm a magician's assistant. Have you ever *not* seen them show their boobs?" Mom tries to get a better look at Pen's costume.

"I'm a dead squirrel, remember?" Pen says. "And we're charging five bucks for admission."

Felix's hitting his bunny ears against his bed. Mom bends down and takes his face in her hands. "You don't have to be a bunny if you don't want to be."

He looks hopeful. "I don't?"

"Nope." She rubs his shoulder. "You can be a dead bunny."

"Dead bunny?" He thinks about it. "Can I have a huge bullet hole between my ears?"

Mom looks at me. I am the bullet-hole expert. "Can you do it for him, Charlie?"

"Sure, kid." I go into my secret Halloween stash, get my bullet-hole kit, wax, and blood, and start making a massive, bloody, goopy hole right in between his ears.

He steps back and checks himself out in the mirror. "Awesome!" he screams, and hugs me. "I can't wait to show my friends."

Friends. Lucky kid.

"Charlie?" Mom tries one last time. "Get dressed."

"Not this time." This time, like my friend Harry, I'd watch from above.

By six it's dark. By seven there's a line down the street to get in. From my window I watch in horror as supernosy people roam the estate, taking pictures. I jealously watch my family live their uncomplicated lives:

156

- Pen's handing out her buttons and gathering signatures.
- Felix and his friends are emptying out all the candy bowls into their bags.
- Mom and Dad are playing host and hostess.

And me, I'm a prisoner in my own room.

I slam my window shut and jump back into my bed and continue streaming my film, *Outcast*. It goes like this:

A beautiful young Indian girl tries to free herself from being an untouchable (like yours truly) by running away. She goes to the capital, starts a promising modeling career, and gets onto *America's Next Top Model*. She wins. Tyra loves her. She thinks she's finally on top of the world. But then someone from her village sees a billboard with her on it. They send a mob to the city, hunt her down, bring her home, and sentence her to death by stoning.

It's an upbeat film, and I can definitely relate. I'm at the part where they're digging the hole to bury her in and the local boys are bringing in the stones to stone her with when suddenly a rock hits my window.

"What the—?" I hit pause and drop to the ground. Then another rock hits.

"Cooper?" Bobby yells up. "You coming down or what?"

I wipe my eyes, blow my nose. Slowly I get to my knees and peek out. He's got on the coolest top hat with attached orange wig ever. And he's wearing a vest, overcoat, floppy tie, short pants, and work boots. "You look awesome." I take it all in. And for a moment I forget my horrible life. "The Mad Hatter from *Alice in Wonderland*, à la Johnny Depp?"

"You got it." Bobby stands back and checks me out. "And you're wearing your pj's?"

"I told you I'm an untouchable."

Bobby flicks the permed wig that's attached to the top hat. "You know why they were called mad hatters?"

I can hear the trick-or-treaters; it makes me want to cry. "Nope."

"Because the chemicals the hat makers used made them all nuts. Crazy." Bobby takes off his hat, checks it out. "And so they called them the mad hatters."

"I like it." I like him.

"Get down here." He stomps the ground, acting like there's no reason to hide.

"No can do."

"Stop feeling sorry for yourself." Bobby takes out a bag of Whoppers and empties them into his mouth.

Word on the street is they're coming—Lillian, Erica, the whole stinking lot of 'em. "Everyone knows, on Halloween, anything goes." They'll TP my house, pour Nair on my hair, spray red dye on my face. I know these things. I did these things.

Kids swirl around him, but he stays right there. Steady as a rock. "Gotta face the music sometime, Cooper."

"Yeah, maybe, but not tonight." Tonight I'm hiding out. No

one's gonna make a public spectacle out of me. "See ya around."
I close the window and jump back on my bed. I get all comfy
and hit play on my computer.

I must have fallen asleep, because when I hear my name being
screamed, the movie's over.

"Charlie Cooper, get down here now!"

I crawl across the floor. I peek out. It's them, the pack of
rabid tweens, led by the mole herself, Greta, dressed like a
witch. And what the heck is she doing here? Don't they believe
in the separation of adults and kids on Halloween?

Behind her are Marta, Lillian, Erica, and of course Babette.
Wait—is Marta wearing a costume or has she had a massive
Hollywood makeover?

I get my binoculars and station myself at the window. I can
barely believe my eyes.

- Her hair is so bleached it looks like a wig/broom.
- Her face is caked with so much makeup she has no expression.
- Her eyes look like she's got a set of baby caterpillars on them.
- Are her lips lined?
- Hold the phone! Is that a cell phone covered in pink rhinestones dangling from her wrist?
- Are those French-tip fake nails?

I gotta admit, if this is real, they got some skills. If it's a costume, she should just keep wearing it for the rest of her life. Marta the Farta has come a long way since I first laid eyes on her three months ago.

"Amazing transformation, don't you agree?" Lillian calls up. "Marta's their big new star. They signed her on the spot."

My heart crumples.

"We are rich," Greta yells into the sky. "America really *is* a beautiful country."

"They love her over there at ABC Family, don't they?" Lillian says.

"Love her," Erica repeats. "She's their new girl. Paying her a fortune, too."

"We just wanted to stop by and tell you," Marta screams up at me, surrounded by her friends, having the night I'd so dreamed of. And then I remember something.

"Hold on a sec," I shout. "Doesn't the pilot shoot the same weekend as the JOs?"

Marta puts her finger up. "I bet you didn't know JOs happen all year long"—she spreads her hands wide—"all over the country."

Lillian drapes her arm over Marta's big shoulders. "Well, they do. And she's our captain. So this one she sits out to do her show, but the next one . . ." They stop to high-five. "Just look at her!" She lifts one arm. "A star and a champ."

Say what? "Really?" I drop to the floor, shaking. Could this be true? Could they really want her on the team?

"You're a plague, Charlie. You take, take, take, and you never—"

"Marta?" Pen cuts her off.

I scramble to my knees, peek over the windowsill, and watch Pen walk over, arms folded across her chest.

"I'm really happy for you, but you should leave."

Marta doesn't say a word. They just stand there, all of them under my window.

"And"—Pen points to Lillian, Erica, and Babs—"take the girls who are pretending to be your friends with you."

"They *are* my friends." Marta pulls them toward her.

She shakes her head. "See you around."

I watch them and think to myself maybe they are real friends now. Maybe I'm the only one incapable of having them.

Bobby walks over, like he's been watching the whole thing. "Wait!" He stops them. "Quick question. What were they calling you until Cooper stopped 'em?"

Silence.

"Marta the Farta," Pen says. "So stop holding their hands like they're your friends."

"And you think she is?" Marta points at the window. I drop low. "She's no friend. I trusted her. I would have done anything for her. She's—" Marta spits.

My mom starts walking over. Erica sees her and pulls Marta. "Time to go."

Lillian and Babs link arms with Marta. "Let's take our celebration back to my house."

I can't believe she's actually letting Marta into her house. I watch them skip away and I feel sick.

"Later, Pen. Mrs. C." Bobby waves and walks off. Mom looks up at me and I wave. Then I collapse on the floor.

Maybe I was wrong. Maybe they do want her on the team. Maybe they realized that with her on the team, they would go further than they've ever gone before. And maybe, just maybe, I am the worst human being out there.

I need candy. Candy helps me solve problems. Shift focus. I get up and crack open my bedroom door. I wait and listen. When I'm sure no one is in the house, I sneak from my room like a criminal. I tiptoe down the stairs and open the door. The first thing I do is check the bowls where Mom dumped all the candy. Empty. Every last one of them. Those little greedy kids.

I spy Felix's bag of candy. Sadly, it's attached to his arm. I have no choice but to revert to old tactics.

His bag of candy is huge. I can feel the spit pool in my mouth just thinking about it. "Felix!" He's with all his friends, sitting under the tree. "Mom sent me to grab all the candy— can you mark your bags?"

His friends move a little farther away from me, like they don't trust me or something.

"If you want to chew on glass or eat rat poison that some

freak put in your candy, then feel free. Just don't come running to me."

Felix's friends band together to discuss. "Okay, fine." Felix hands me the most bounteous booty you've ever seen. "But Charlie, I swear to God, I'm gonna get you if you take any."

"Only suspicious ones." I carry it up to my bedroom and get to work. Definition of *suspicious*? Everything with gross nuts.

Pen knocks while I'm in the zone. "Charlie?"

I'm quick to answer. "By all things holy, Pen, leave me alone." Lock door. Take out all candy with peanut butter, coconut flakes, and finally almonds. Gross. Apples, toothbrushes go into same pile. Now I divide that up and put it back in their bags. The good stuff goes inside my pillowcase. I run downstairs. The boys are under the tree, their eyes glued to the door. When they see me, they jump up.

I hand them the bags. "Lucky for you I got it in time, or that tongue of yours—" I point. "Gone!" They scream and run.

My good deed for the night has been done. I head back in, take a shower, and tuck into my bed. The sweet smell of candy finds my nose and brings me such joy. Outside, the grown-ups are getting louder, the owls and bats hoot and screech, and all I can taste is sweet, sweet stolen chocolate. I think this is what Dr. Scales means when he says you make your happiness.

The Reinvention
of Marta the Farta

First day back at school. The YouTube video of my downfall
has 257,000 hits and counting. I'm a star.

I stand in front of my closet, wondering what kind of
clothes you're supposed to wear on the day the entire school
is going to rejoice in your failure, kick you when you're down,
smash your face in your own humiliation. It takes careful
consideration.

I think about Imelda Marcos. The first lady of the Phil-
ippines. She had over three thousand pairs of shoes. They
brought her to trial on corruption charges. The people hated
her, of course. She had all those Jimmy Choos and they had
no food. I wonder which pair she wore when she went to
trial.

TRUE FACT: Who cares about food when you've got Jimmy Choos?

Did she go low-key, cheap flats, or did she go for her most extravagant, in-your-face Jimmy Choos?

After much thought, I go for low-key. My faded, ripped vintage Levi's, black tank, and lumberjack flannel. I roll the legs up and pair with a set of black leather high-top Converse tennis shoes with studs. Hair down, black glasses on, deep breath.

My heart pounds like crazy when I walk into the classroom. Mr. L's got his orcas cooing in the background. But not even those sweet whales can stop me from wondering what horrible thing will happen to me today. I channel Jai's words on the untouchables and try to be detached. If you're detached, they can't hurt you, right?

But Marta didn't come to school today. She doesn't come for the rest of the week either. And man, did the class feel weird. It was like all the energy that buzzed in that room was gone. One good thing—the back row of girls didn't seem to care at all about me anymore. And I didn't care about them. A major relief.

But then on the following Monday, when I'm looking out at the rain and Mr. L is pulling up his tube socks, the door opens and Marta catwalks in like a Victoria's Secret model in her tackiest gear.

Mr. L drops his favorite mug. It shatters on the floor and he doesn't even realize. That's how different she looks. "Ms.

Urloff?" he stutters. "Is that you? What—"

Even I have to admit she's a vision of put-together sparkle. The entire room stops what they're doing and stares at her. She throws Bobby a high five. Her nails are at least four inches long, pointed and fake. I'm so jealous. They immediately make room for her in the back row. She doesn't even glance in my direction. She is unrecognizable.

"Hey, Marta!" Lillian coos. "You look so hot! Those platform sneaks are the bomb!"

Marta's rockin' the bright-purple Juicy Couture rhinestone tracksuit. Her hair is bleached and straightened.

"Oh, my God, where did you get that? Juicy Couture? Those nails? That hair?" They gather around her like birds.

"Is that from the set? Is your driver here?" Even the dorks huddle around her.

Bobby glances in my direction, but I do my best not to show that it's irritating the heck out of me.

BECAUSE LET'S FACE IT: Except for the horrible attitude and the bad taste, she was exactly where I thought I was going to be at the very beginning of this depressing installment of my so-called life.

"You've missed a lot of school, Marta." Mr. L takes a deep breath; he's concerned. "We have covered so much, I am worried for you."

166

I turn to see her response. The old Marta would have cared. But the new Marta doesn't even carry a backpack, just a bag stamped with as many Louis Vuitton logos as can fit. She shrugs, like *whatever*.

Mr. L implores her. "How will you make up your assignments?"

She taps her purple fake nails against the desk.

"A tutor, a course." She smells like powder.

The whole class goes, "Ah, man! A tutor on set! She is so lucky."

I personally feel like throwing up. It's all I want and I'll never have.

Mr. L walks back over to her desk and looks down at her. "I'll give your tutor the curriculum. What's his email?"

"Don't know yet. The producers are working on it." She shrugs, as in *Get off my back*.

"Marta." Mr. L's not going for it. "Be sure you have a tutor. Otherwise you'll fall way behind and you'll have to repeat seventh grade."

Marta rolls her eyes again. "Oh, please!" She looks at her sharpened, shiny nails. "No offense, Mr. L, but I'm never gonna need any of that stuff."

"True that!" Erica throws up a high five. Babs reaches out to slap her.

"She's going all the way!" Lillian moves closer to her.

Marta is a massive celebrity at Happy Canyon. Her black

town car waits for her in a handicapped spot in the parking lot all day long. Kids from kindergarten to high school flock to her; teachers ask her to come and speak. She is an inspiration, they tell her.

I follow her like an invisible ant. I notice things about her, new things, like:

- She needs no one.
- She avoids Coach and the multi-purpose room, where the gym team practices, like the plague.
- Her new perfume is horrible.

Being invisible has its perks. I picked up on patterns. Such as: Whenever Marta showed up at school, Lillian, Erica, and even big-boobed Lola kissed her butt like there was no tomorrow. They pretended to be her best friend, painted her nails at lunch, showered her with compliments. They barely mentioned the JOs. "It's so boring," they'd whine. "No one is even going to this one," I'd hear them say. "I so wish we could get out of it." Marta, she didn't suspect a thing. And why should she? They were acting like the kind of friends I longed for.

But the second Marta took off in her fancy car, Lillian, Lola, and Erica would disappear into the gym and train harder than I'd ever seen them train before. The upcoming Junior Olympics was all they talked about. They were obsessed with it. They acted like it was going to be *the* highlight of their careers.

It bothered me. In my gut I knew they were up to something.

Then one day Mr. L's going on about the lost gold in the Laurel Canyon caves again, and the door suddenly flies opens.

Coach is bright red. He storms in. His eyes on one person. "Marta Urloff!" He points. "Now!"

"Coach, what's going on?" Lillian looks seriously concerned.

Erica raises her hand. "We'll come too."

"Yeah, we're a team." Lillian and Lola jump up.

"You sit," he commands. "Marta, up."

I'm hoping with all my might that Coach talks some sense into her. But only minutes pass before Marta comes back. Her eyes are red. She's been crying.

"What happened?" Lillian puts her hand on Marta's shoulder and squeezes.

"I quit the team," she announces.

"You did what?" Lillian's voice trembles with satisfaction.

"I quit," Marta says again.

"No!" Erica smiles.

The room goes silent. I can't shake the feeling that all this is part of some plan and Marta doesn't even know it.

Bobby turns. "As in you quit the team?"

"As in no more team for me and no more school." She looks around. Her confidence is incredible. "Or didn't you all hear? I am going to be a TV star."

Lillian's smiling.

"What about the JOs?" Mr. L asks. "You were so excited—"

"JOs happen all the time," she answers flatly.

Lillian is suddenly positive. "That's true. All the time."

Erica looks at Lillian. "Shooting a pilot!" she gasps. "Now that's a once-in-a-lifetime thing."

I feel it in my bones. "You're making a mistake."

Marta stops dead in her tracks and looks down at me. Her nostrils are huge, red, and flaring. There's not enough concealer and mascara to hide the fact that she looks like a bull about to charge. "Let me guess—you think I should give you the pilot and go to the JOs—"

"Uh, yes! I do!" I shout. This is all going so horribly wrong for her.

Bobby slaps my desk. "Charlie, shut your mouth."

Lillian nods. "Guess why."

A kid in the second row asks, "Wasn't Charlie the one who tried to steal the TV show?"

"Exactly." Erica gives him a high five.

"They call her the scorpion," he whispers so loudly they can hear him down the hall.

"If it wasn't for Lillian"— they point to her—"she'd still just be Marta the Farta."

TRUE FACT: I'm officially the worst human being here.

170

"Quiet." Mr. L's face goes red. He is pissed. "Leave Charlie alone."

"Leave her alone?" The third row laughs. "Not a problem."

"Oh, she's gonna be alone, all right!"

I look at Bobby, willing him to say something. To tell them to shut up. To tell them to get off my back. One word from him and they'd stop. But Bobby just pulls his hood over his head. I guess some things are just too hard to go against.

I hear Babs's voice in the background. "She's kinda like the ugly dog at the pound no one wants, right?"

I feel my entire body shrink. Then I freeze. I feel doomed. Jai's words no longer help. Calling Dr. Scales! Calling Dr. Scales! The ship—my ship, me—we're all sinking. And just when I think I can't move because of the humiliation, I hear Bobby's voice echoing through my brain.

"Says the girl who'd jump off a cliff if Lillian told her to. Who are you to talk? Who are any of you to talk?"

The room fills with a heavy quiet, like the one you feel inside when you know you're wrong. I look at Bobby's beautiful profile. He looks back at me and winks. The hood goes back up.

He's on my side still.

Pickler Calling

At lunchtime, I'm summoned to Pickler's office—which, for once, is a good thing. See, Mr. L locked up his classroom today because he had to leave, so I had no place to eat lunch but the bathroom. Yeah, that's right, the bathroom.

The door's open. "Come in." He points to the chair. He has a big drop of yogurt on his upper lip. "So." He leans back in his chair, stretches his arms over his head, totally not aware of the mess on his face. "You have any news for me?"

"Nope."

He cocks his head to the side. "Nothing about Marta Urloff dropping out of the team, pulling out of the JOs because she has to act in some dead-end TV show?"

"You heard."

Pickler hits the desk so hard, he hurts his hand. "She's got it in her head that she can train on set and become so rich and famous that they'll beg her to go to the Olympics." Pickler blinks like he's going crazy. "Is she nuts? Has someone taken hold of her brain?"

Yes. Lillian. Lillian has taken hold of her brain. The conversation loops in my head, but this time I see what she's doing.

TRUE FACT: Lillian is way smarter than I am.

Lillian: "What if I was to tell you that you'd pull out of the JOs all by yourself?"

Marta: "I'd tell you that you're insane."

I look at Pickler. "Lillian. Lillian's behind it."

"Lillian?"

"Lillian told Marta she'd pull out of the JOs all by herself. Marta never believed her, of course. Who would? I mean, Marta wanted the JOs more than anything in the world."

"And you"—he glares—"got me to pay for them. Now I'm out three grand."

"But here she is pulling out of the JOs *all by herself*. Lillian did it. She wants to be captain."

"Well, Marta's a fool." Pickler picks up the phone. "She's out. Lillian's in." He shoos me out of his office. "I'm done with her."

But I can't be. "Let me try one more time, please."

Pickler puts the phone down. "I need an answer by the end of today."

I walk across the upper yard. It feels like a hostile place now. I know where to find her—at the cool table, next to Lillian and Erica, the two girls whose entire reason for being is to make Marta fail. Talk about dream stealers. When they see me coming, they all stop talking. They turn and stare. The scorpion jokes start coming, but by now they've lost their sting.

"Marta?" I call her name. "Can I have a word, please?"

She doesn't even turn around.

There is no noise except my heart pounding. "In private, please."

Marta stuffs her lunch back into the brown bag. It's the exact same lunch she's always eaten, which makes me think that her aunt isn't even making lunch for her. A criminal offense, in the Book of Charlie.

"Get lost." Erica shoos me away like a dirty fly.

Lillian pops blueberries into her mouth. She's taunting me. "Marta, who told you about the audition?"

"My friends." Lillian and Erica throw her high fives.

"You ever ask yourself why all of a sudden they're such good friends?"

"Please, not this again." Lillian stands up. But I'm not afraid of Lillian. What else can she do to me that she hasn't already done? I'm an untouchable, remember?

Erica comes at me. Now, Erica . . . Erica I'm afraid of. I

start backing away. But then, out of the blue I hear my favorite voice of all.

"Erica, back off." Bobby comes walking over.

I wait until he's close enough to pull her off in case she lunges at me.

"What have they wanted all along?" I try to get closer so Marta sees just how sure of this I am. Lillian looks like she's gonna stab me with her plastic fork. I continue, my voice even stronger than before. "They wanted you off the team. And now you're *off* the team." For the first time, she turns around.

"It's temporary. And I chose it," Marta replies. "So technically they didn't get anything they wanted."

I try again. "Remember when she said that you'd pull out of the JOs on your own?"

Marta's eyes narrow. She's thinking back. "Yeah." She nods. "That was weird, right?"

"No, what's weird is—she was right. She called it." I am sweating hard and my mouth is as dry as a dead man's, but this is it, one last try. "You're out of the JOs. You, Marta, pulled out on your own. Don't you get it?"

"Go away. Just go." Lillian glances over at Marta, and for the first time, Marta looks confused. I can see it in her eyes. Doubt. Yes, Marta! Yes! She's getting it.

"Don't you see this was her plan all along? Lillian's captain now—Pickler just told me." There's a flash in her eyes when she hears the news. I think I may be getting through to her.

But then, dang it, the bell rings, and Lillian snaps up Marta's arm and whispers in her ear. I keep at it. "Just tell Pickler today that you're still on the team and you're going, all right? That's all I want."

They huddle together, Lillian and Erica whispering into both of her ears until they've filled them up with their lies. And then, to make matters worse, I hear someone sing Katy Perry. Katy Perry makes me want to punch walls.

The three of them get up and start walking toward class. I'm left standing in the rapidly deserted upper yard watching Marta walk away. I catch Bobby just before he starts up the stairs. "Bobby!"

"Your girlfriend's calling," Skip teases.

"Give it a rest, Skip." Bobby shoves his hands into his pockets, pulls up his hood, and drops his head. "What's up, Cooper?"

I take his wrists and pull him away from his idiot friends. We reach the bottom of the stairs, and I whisper in his ear, "We have to get her off that show."

Bobby rolls his eyes. "Enough, Coop. Maybe they're right and you're wrong—ever thought of that?" The bell rings and Bobby goes running off to class.

Yeah, I thought about it. But I know better.

Can I Really Be
That Wrong?

"I must be missing something," I say to Pen after school. "They keep saying these JOs don't matter, but I've never seen Lillian, Erica, and Lola practice so hard in my life. That's all they do." I take a deep breath and pull my hair up into a bun. "But not when Marta's around. When she's at school, they don't go near the gym." I toss a ball at the wall.

"You think they're playing her?" Pen asks.

"Yeah." From the bottom of my heart. They're scheming.

"But wouldn't she know everything about gymnastics?" Pen points out. "It's her life."

"I've thought about that long and hard. Marta's basically computer illiterate. She isn't up on schedules or the fine details, the rules and regulations of that world. And her mother never trained in the US."

She points to my laptop. "You know what to do."

Up until now, I've avoided it because the world of gymnastics is convoluted and creepy. But this afternoon, I put a big cheese pizza in the oven for me alone and I go online to understand what Lillian and Erica were up to. It takes some time to navigate my way through the craziness of it all. But three hours later I crack it. "Bingo!" I feel weak in the knees, both sickened and thrilled at the same time. "So I'm not the meanest girl in the world after all," I mumble as I read.

Mom turns away from the stove. "What did you just say?"

My eyes linger on the lines. "They're not just shutting her out of the team. They're ruining her life."

Mom gives me a blank stare. "Go on."

I read it aloud. "'The JO meet this weekend *is* unique because it's the *last* one of the season, and it's a level-ten qualifying meet.'"

"Translation please." Mom's suddenly serious.

I hit my head against the table but I am smiling. "If she doesn't go and qualify, she'll miss the cut-off for the next Olympics, which means that instead of going in at sixteen, she has to go in at twenty. It's a *career ender.*"

TRUE FACT: Jai wasn't kidding when he was talking about the ripples in the pond.

178

Mom looks shocked. "And they know this?"

"I'd bet my life on it."

Mom goes back to kneading the dough. "You have to tell her."

I could say the house was on fire and she'd accuse me of saying it to steal back the part. "She'll never listen to me."

"She might listen to this." Mom points to the screen. "If she doesn't, then you've done all you can."

But no, I haven't, I scream inside. Because it's my fault. All of it. And if she loses out on the Olympics, it's because of me, not them.

I walk outside, kick some rocks. Then I go down to the fence and look over. Across the way, the green meadow with boulders and grass is calling my name. If only Bobby was there, throwing bottles against the rocks. I could definitely use some good bottle throwing about now.

The Stalking of Marta the Farta

The next day after school, I wait for her in the parking lot. Friday is the only day she takes the bus home. At 3:15, she walks past me.

"Marta!" I call after her. She keeps walking like I don't exist. I run after her and finally catch up. "I have to talk to you."

Her hair is so straight, it looks like a doll's. She's wearing a short leather jacket and boots. Rhinestones on both, of course. She stops abruptly, halfway down the road. "Oh, so now you want to be my friend?"

"Not exactly."

"Please." She puts both her hands on her hips. "Everyone

wants to be my friend now. And when the show airs, I will have so many 'friends' asking me for stuff, I won't have any more stuff."

This is what fame does to you, people.

She starts walking again.

"Hey!" I scream. "I'm just gonna say one last thing, and then you'll never hear from me again."

She stops. Turns. "I'm all ears."

"You know the JOs you're missing this weekend happen to be the *last* of the level-ten nationals? Do you know what that means?" I pause, waiting for the word *last* to sink into her brain. But there's no sign of it. "Marta, don't you get it? If you miss this, you miss qualifying."

"You're lying. It's not the last."

I laugh. "Yes it is. And it's not me who's been lying to you. It's them. They've been tricking you all along."

"So what if it is the last, who cares? Chad will work his magic, break the rules, and get me in," she yells back at me like my words are pebbles being tossed at a window. They're not getting in.

"You," I repeat loudly. "You care, Marta." I implore, "You miss this, and you'll miss out on the Olympics in four years. You'll have to wait until you're twenty, Marta! Twenty! You'll be old. Done." For a second, Marta's face changes, like there's doubt. So I go in for the kill. "Your mother's dream, Marta. Gone."

A wicked grin like a mask appears. "TV, Charlie, that's the new dream. My mom had a medal, but she ended up working in a bagel shop—you said it yourself."

Dang it, I did.

"I'm living her dream, right now." She tosses her head back. "On set I train with the best coach money can buy. If I want to go to the JOs, I'll go. They can fix it. Everything can be fixed when you've got a hit show. Chad tells me every day. Hah!" she says like a crazy lady. "Gone are the days when I have to beg. Gone are the days when I have to plead. Now I have a driver, Charlie." Her eyes are huge. "Do you realize that? My own driver. I have more money than I can balance in my checkbook. I never, ever have to ask anyone for anything again. Including you. Oh, by the way, Chad got me a work permit in an hour. I didn't even have to go down there. And . . ." She glares at me. "We're moving to Beverly Hills. So take that and suck on it."

Well, this went worse than I thought. It's almost impossible to believe it's the same girl who used to eat tuna in the bathroom. But you know what? If I look hard, I can still see her in there, the girl in the bathroom. So I try one last time. I yell down the street, "What's gonna happen to you if the show gets canceled?"

"Canceled, hah!" Marta skips off. Invincible. Untouchable. And I realize I can't help her. Bobby's right. It's time to let go.

What Goes Up
Must Come Down

On Monday, in preparation for the annual Thanksgiving trip
to the Santa Barbara Mission, we're in class talking about how
the white man destroyed the Native Americans when Pickler
comes barging in. "I'm going to need Lillian, Erica, and Lola,
please."

Mr. L jumps up. He hates being interrupted by Pickler
more than anything. "But, but . . ." He's all flustered. "We're
in the middle of discussing white man's genocide of the Native
American."

Pickler shrugs. "It can wait. But the team photo cannot.
The team must carry on!" Pickler sings. "And these girls will
take us to the top. Isn't that right, girls?"

"Yeah!" They cheer for themselves. Typical. The new team. No Marta. Lillian is captain, Erica second-in-command, Lola third. They've never looked happier. They march out of the room like perfectly oiled wind-up dolls. "May I have a word with you outside, please?" Mr. L eyes Pickler.

Pickler rolls his eyes. "Can't it wait?"

"No." Mr. L opens the door. "Class, I'll be gone for five minutes. Silent reading, please."

The moment the door shuts, I look at Bobby. "What's that about?"

Bobby looks over at Marta's empty seat. "Mr. L's got a soft spot for her."

I'm about to move in a little closer when jerk-to-the-stars Skip walks by and kicks my chair. "Yo, Charlie, your crazy animal-loving sister give up yet?" Turns out Lola's dad is the one who's building the animal-killing mansions on Stanley Hills Drive, and Skip likes her, so he's going all macho. He kicks my chair again.

"She'll never give up." I feel a strange surge of pride for my sister. "Especially when she's protecting lives way more valuable than yours."

He's about to kick it again when the door flies open and hits the wall. Mr. L storms in, fuming. "It seems the team will not wait for Marta." He takes a deep breath, and his nostrils flare like a bull's. "So where were we?"

184

"The big and powerful taking advantage of the poor and weak?" I ask.

He eyes the third row. "Yes, I'm afraid that's exactly where we are."

Acceptance

That afternoon, I find myself completely alone. After all, both Felix and Pen are popular—they have lots of stuff to do. And me, I literally have two friends in the world. And one of them lives in Mumbai. I peek out the window and see my father laughing with his workers. I see the workers laughing with each other. I dust off the blender, open the freezer, and rummage through it until I find what I need.

One pint of vanilla ice cream.

Frozen pineapple, mango, banana, and the magic ingredient, Cool Whip.

I whip it all up, pour it into a tall glass, and Skype Jai. "Yo! Jai!" I can't hide my happiness when I see him. "Where have you been?" And then I notice his surroundings. Instead of being surrounded by tons and tons of homeless people, he's surrounded by the beach, by swaying palm trees and sand. I grab the screen. "What the heck? Where are you?"

"Hello, Charlie!" All I see are teeth—that's how much he's smiling. "Forgive the tardy response, my kind friend, but we have moved the entire family."

Tall and skinny trees, swaying in the breeze, and sand so white I need my shades. "Where?"

He shakes his head. "I am not at liberty to discuss."

I'm suddenly freezing cold. I know what he means, right off the bat. The Russians found him. They've been after him ever since he hacked into President Vladimir Putin's personal computer and gave the information to the British secret service. "They found you?"

"Damn that *60 Minutes*!" Jai curses. "But my employers relocated us safely." He points to the ocean. "Now the family is enjoying the time away from the city." He's trying to sound calm, but I know from experience that he's not. Who can be calm when the Russian secret police are after you?

"Why did you do it?"

"I am sorry to admit, money, Charlie. I needed the money." He looks down, then back at me. "Please don't look at me that way. It was also for a good cause. The man is a real thief. But the money was an amount I could not in good conscience turn down."

"What do the Russians want from you?"

"I assume the information I relieved from his computer." Jai rolls his eyes.

I'm guessing it painted a less-than-flattering portrait of President Putin—not that anyone would accuse the dude of being an angel. "Are you okay?"

"I'm very well protected. In fact," he teases, "this computer will self-destruct unless you start telling me about your Holly-wood career."

I'd way rather talk about Putin, sip my Cool Whip smoothie, and lie back against my pillows. "It's over, Jai. Done."

"The Hollywood career?" He leans into the screen like he's getting all up in my grille on a virtual level. "But, but you were going to be the next Hannah Montana. My sisters were already telling their friends—"

"What?" I'm momentarily so horrified by the image of her butt that I forget about the whole torched-middle-school-image thing.

"Fame can be very destructive." He throws it out there like a hook I'm supposed to grab and run with.

"I don't care." I stick out my lip and stare at the wall, 'cause you know what? I want to be famous. Is that so bad?

"No, it's not," Jai says.

Wait a sec. "I didn't say anything."

"But you thought it." He winks. "I can read your thoughts."

I laugh. But Jai's not laughing. "Wait, can you?"

Jai laughs. "No, Charlie, but I know you. I know what it

is you want." That's when he gives me a look. "So what's your plan?"

"I'm out," I announce.

Jai narrows his eyes. "You're giving up?"

I lie down on my stomach so the screen's right in front of me. Jai lies down on the beach so he's on the sand and the laptop's right in front of him. It feels like we're two friends staying up past our bedtime. "My plan is to not care. To take a complete break from caring." I wipe my nose. "Then maybe I'll care again one day, but I'm not sure. My life is a wreck." I remember what Mom said to me in the car. "And it's all my fault." There, I said it. I admitted it. It's in me.

Jai says nothing for a long time. Nothing's worse than the old I-told-you-so.

"You know what I do when everything feels like it's crashing down on me?" The mask of calm on Jai's face slips. "I swim. I swim until I have swum so far I can barely see the shore." He turns the laptop out to the endless sea. "My lungs burn, my legs feel like weights, and my mouth is full of the taste of salt. I don't know if I can make it back. I play games with myself about what would happen, where would I go, who would I become without the burden of my family to provide for? I realize, no one. And then I swim back, too tired to be mad, or sad or vengeful. My sister provides me with a cup of chai, and I am once again accepting of my world."

I stare at the screen, at the emptiness of the Arabian Sea. I can see it. I can see him, fighting against the waves, struggling to get out, away. And then turning around and struggling to get back in.

"But I have nothing to come back to." I've destroyed everything. "It's too hard, Jai."

Jai nods like he's already considered this. "Life must be measured in smaller moments, Charlie, to achieve satisfaction. It's not *being* the Hollywood star. It's *becoming* the Hollywood star. It's what you do along the way. That is what your life is."

I think of what my life is, and besides Bobby, there's nothing left. My whole raison d'être—fame and fortune—is gone.

"There's always something to swim back for." He watches me. "Ah, I see a smile. Is there a someone in your life?"

I'm starting to sweat. "No."

He grins from ear to ear. "Is there someone I should be jealous about?"

Did he just read my mind again? "No way, Jai. No one." No way was I gonna tell him. "I am totally, one hundred percent—"

"Charlie?" Dad knocks. "May I come in?"

Jai hears him and waves. "All right, I will leave you. Good-bye, Charlie."

"Stay safe, Jai," I say, and feel a jolt at how quickly his face disappears from my life. "Hey, Dad." I look up.

He sits on my bed and gives me one of those deep-thoughts looks. "Heard you had another rough day."

190

I take out a Sharpie and start to draw on my leg through the tights. I feel his eyes on me waiting for me to talk. It makes me *not* want to talk at all.

Felix starts calling. "Dad! Is Dad up there?" Felix screams from downstairs. "Dad, anywhere, Dad?"

I stop drawing and look up, grateful. "I think you're wanted."

"Down in a second," Dad yells back. He sits on my bed, looks around. "Hey, where'd Mandela and Jobs go?"

I shrug. Hoping he won't push.

"Okay." He stands. "I get it—you need space. You're close to being a teenager."

TRUE FACT: I know I was supposed to be pouty, but the words "close to being a teenager" made me want to jump up and sing.

"Charlie, baby?" Mom comes running up the stairs, knocks on the door. "You have a call."

I glance at my watch. It's after ten. "Who could that be?" And why are they letting me talk this late?

"A friend?" Dad looks hopeful. "See, you *do* have a friend!"

Help me.

I'm getting a bad feeling. "Who is it?"

Mom gets this weird half smile. She shakes her head. "It's Chad." She hands me the phone. "He says it's urgent."

Oh, God, Chad. The last person I ever want to talk to

again. This guy is like the silverback gorilla baby poacher of Hollywood. That's the way I see him now. He poaches up all these little babies, uses them, and spits them out. I take a deep breath, arm myself for what I know is trouble.

"Charlie Cooper, how the hell are you?"

This is a man who didn't even pick up the phone to apologize to me. This is the man who purposely humiliated me by sending that horrible car with that stinky driver. This is a man who cared about no one. And in spite of all that I still feel the same excitement.

"First of all, no hard feelings, right, kid? It's the nature of the beast."

Mom and Dad are watching my every move. I slip into the bathroom to be alone. I lean up against the wall and take a deep breath. "What do you want?"

"Major problem, as in 'Houston, we have a problem.'"

"I don't know what that means—"

He cuts me off. "Come on, you never watched *Apollo 13*?"

"Nope." Sounds old. And boring.

"True story." He keeps on going, like I care. "When the entire spaceship is about to blow and the pilot calls control, which is in Houston, right? He's about to die, right? But when he calls, he says supercalmly, 'Houston, we have a problem.'"

"Gotcha." Whatever. I leave the bathroom and walk down the hallway. Halfway down the stairs I see Pen and Felix. Felix is drawing a comic, and Pen is editing the footage she had from the rally that day. Skip was there. Lola, Lillian, and Erica, of course, showed up in their Bentley to run over the protesters. They didn't have a chance against a Bentley.

"Well, Charlie, we got a problem." He laughs. "And her name is Marta."

I stop and sit. I always knew this moment would come. Why? Because Marta is Marta. She's tough. She's inflexible. Stubborn as heck and hates using deodorant. I walk back up and head into the bathroom. "Sorry, Chad, Marta doesn't talk to me anymore." I pick up a pair of tweezers and start plucking my nostril hairs. The pain makes me want to kill him less.

"Well, she's a monster. And worse—she's a terrible actress. And when I say terrible, I don't mean good terrible. I mean horrible terrible. Why the heck didn't you warn me?"

"I tried to. At the very beginning, I told you." I pull out a chunk of hair and a small piece of skin.

"I made a mistake, all right? I'm only human."

My eyes water. "No, you're not."

"All right, fine, I'm not." He sounds like he's going to burst into tears, but Chad doesn't have tears, so I know it's just an act and I am so not falling for it. "Oh, Charlie, please, please, help. I'm begging you."

I'm not going to lie—listening to him grovel is almost as much fun as shopping at the Salvation Army.

"It wasn't even my fault. See, when I told the producers you lied to keep her from getting the part, they immediately

193

thought she was the victim. Marta!" he yells. "See, victims are majorly in right now. Especially dorky ones who can work the beam like she can. They thought you were the bully. Bullies are out. Especially bullies who aren't so good on the beam."

"I don't know why you're telling me this," I interject.

"So here was this down-and-out kid who was picked on by everyone. Lillian told me the whole story about how you and all your mean girlfriends called her Marta the Farta and how you made her life unlivable."

She's good. I gotta hand it to her. "So go find someone else."

"The producers thought she was this swan in the body of a really ugly duckling, and they wanted to show that change. But, and here's the kicker—" He starts his fake whining again. "She never *changed* into the dang swan. She's a monster, kid, a total monster. And we've got to get rid of her, pronto."

"Marta's a gymnast, not an actress. I tried to tell you." I'm tired of talking about this. I start plucking my eyebrows. "There's nothing I can do for you."

"It's not what *you* can do for me," Chad announces. "Charlie, it's what *I* can do for you."

I put down the tweezers and sit on the toilet. "The way I see it, we're done, Chad."

"Oh, no, we're not." He pauses so long I think he's hung up. "We want *you*, Charlie Cooper. We want you back. The first choice. The only choice."

"Me?" My legs go weak, like two noodles.

"And to show you how sincerely sorry we are, this is what I'm prepared to do. First, I'll send a limo. A Hummer. With a pool. You want a pool, right?"

"A pool?" I roll it around a little. "Pools are good."

"To your door, first thing tomorrow morning. I'll messenger scripts to you now. Skip school. You'll have a tutor. Word of honor."

My heart throbbed in spite of my iron will. He just outlined my dream.

"Charlie? I know you can do it. I've seen you. You are Josie."

Freeze. I want to savor this moment. Savor it, revel in it.

"Charlie, really? You want me to beg—"

I do, of course. I want him to beg. I want to be showered with chocolates. I want to be loved and adored. "Yes, Chad, beg. Beg me."

"I'll send the contract over ASAP. We will sign you tonight. You will receive your first check tomorrow. You will be able to live in Beverly Hills. Your face will be all over town—on buses, on billboards. You will be famous."

In the distance, I see Houdini looking right at me. Some of us are chosen to do great things. It's our destiny. No matter what knocks we take, nothing can derail us. Why? Because you just can't mess with destiny. Houdini knew it, and I know it too.

Chad's voice cuts through my head. "You know you want this."

I do. I want it so bad I can taste it.

Field Trip

Lucky me—today's our super depressing field trip to the Santa Barbara Mission, where we learn about how the Mexicans and the local Native Americans were all enslaved and killed by the Spaniards just to make these missions. A lot of the kids think the teachers are lying, because their parents told them that the church took such good care of all the locals.

Lillian and Erica are applying yet another layer of lip gloss while we stand in line for the bus. Bobby's suddenly at my side. He nudges me. "Hey, you want to ride together?" He checks me out. "You look sharp."

Even I have to admit my camo jacket looks majorly swag. Especially when paired with tight black jeans and Docs. We line up next to each other and file onto the bus. We take seats—me by the window and Bobby looking over my shoulder. We pull out of school, up Laurel Canyon, past our house. Bobby sees the mansion my dad's restoring from the window. From the tall bus, you can make out the whole thing through the giant trees that block the property from view. "It's three floors, just like the original Walker place. There's gonna be a ballroom too. Majorly cool."

"Do I get a personal tour sometime?" He nudges me with his shoulder.

"Absolutely." The tingling hits my innards before I even finish the line.

The bus chugs up the hill and drops into the valley that's as hot as a stove. We get on the freeway, deal with some majorly bad mojo on the 101 North.

Bobby's just bouncing in the seat, enjoying the ride. His body is warm. I am mesmerized by the way our thighs jiggle. When we hit the water, it's so bright and so beautiful, a smile takes hold. "My dad came back." He wipes his hands on his jeans but never takes his eyes off the beautiful Santa Barbara coastline. "He says he'll stop with the bad stuff."

"That's awesome, Bobby."

"And he's working again, painting and sculpting in the garage. It feels like the old days." He looks a thousand pounds lighter. The hood's off, *and* his eyes are bright and happy.

His hand is right next to mine, waiting, just waiting for me to grab it. I so want to hold his hand. I glance down again. It's just sitting there, doing nothing. The butterflies are back. Suddenly sweat covers my hand. I quickly put it between my legs to dry it. The moment's gone.

We sit and watch the ocean go by. In the back kids are talking trash, sharing headphones, yelling at the driver about which way he should be going while tossing Cheetos in people's hair. But Bobby and I are rows up, quiet and happy, lost in our own worlds. Really happy. After a while he reaches over and touches my hand. Then he links his fingers through mine. I almost have a heart attack.

Bobby nods slowly. "You're okay, Cooper."

I have no idea what that means. Does it mean we're going out? "Thanks, Bobby," I say quietly. We both keep staring out the window like a couple of old people.

Who's supposed to pull their hand away first? Or are we just supposed to stay like this until the bus comes to a stop? And what if someone sees? Do we pull away before, or is this the way we announce we're dating? If only I had a normal older sister who had actually dated before me so she could help me with all this. I'm in such a panic, I don't even see Lillian until she's hovering over us like a black shadow.

"You two are looking mighty cozy." Her long hair falls down like two sheets.

I pull my hand away. "Go away, Lillian."

"Don't stop holding hands on my account." She smiles, then

bends so low that Bobby's head is almost inside her blouse. "So sad about Marta."

She's gonna ruin everything. I get a pang in my stomach and turn away from her. But Bobby lifts his hand and pushes her away like she's totally insignificant. "Go away."

"But great news for you, Charlie, right?" Lillian says.

"Leave." I know what she came here to do.

Bobby's suddenly interested. "What are you talking about?"

"Oh, come on, Charlie didn't tell you the good news?" Her mouth drops. "Marta's out, and . . . wait for it, wait for it . . ." She points right at me. "Charlie's in."

Bobby moves away from me like I suddenly stink. "Is that true?"

"Yeah, but—" I stop and look for a sign that he will listen to me. None comes.

"Bravo!" Lillian starts to clap. "I mean really, bravo." She cuts me off before I can finish. "I have to hand it to you. I am impressed. Talk about long-term scheming. You finally got it, didn't you, Charlie? The role you'd do anything to get."

"If anyone gets the scheming award, it's you." But the minute I say it, I realize that it's Marta who's lost everything in this battle between us. She's the real victim here.

Bobby looks at her, at me. He shakes his head in disgust.

"Get to your seat, please." The bus driver gets on his speaker. "No standing in the bus while it's moving."

"Enjoy the rest of the ride." Lillian walks to her seat at the very back of the bus, where all of her kind sit and plot their next mean move.

Suddenly everything is still. It's all changed. Bobby isn't talking. And neither am I. We're past Carpentaria when he says, "I want to tell you that I—"

I cut him off before he has the chance to say something that's going to hurt. "Chad called me last night. Told me Marta's out. I had nothing to do with it. Ask my parents."

"Why?"

"Apparently she's out of control. And she sucks."

Bobby wipes his hands on his jeans. "And they offered it to you."

"Yes."

"And what did you say?"

I look out the window. It's so complicated. I barely slept the night before. "They're going to give it to someone, Bobby." I pause before I let it drop. "So why not me?"

Bobby shakes his head like he knew it all along. Like I'm bad. "So you took it?"

Our eyes meet. I'm trying to figure out how to put it when he gets up and says, "I should have known."

I watch him. He walks up the aisle and takes a seat next to the driver. About as far from me, Lillian, Erica, and Lola as he can get. I guess he thinks I'm no different than they are.

Marta's Fall

The next morning, the day they leave for the JOs, everyone knows about Marta. It's all over Instagram. It's all over Facebook, Twitter, and the trades. Marta Urloff was let go. Terminated. Fired. There are pictures of her demise.

- Marta walking out of the place wearing her old clothes, head down, like she just lost everything in a fire.
- Studio security wrestling Greta for the keys to the Mercedes convertible she's been driving around in.
- Greta belting the security guy with her new LV bag.
- Security taking said LV bag.

It's all anyone can talk about. But as soon as the bell rings, Mr. L claps loudly. "Settle down." He wags his finger. "Let us not delight in someone's fall." He walks around his desk, about to start the Gratitude Prayer, when the door opens.

The entire room gasps. It's like seeing a ghost. Marta is standing in the middle of the doorway, looking like a zombie in her old pink velour outfit. Swollen eyes, so red and puffy you can barely see her eyeballs. Red nose. Chapped lips, pale skin, and knotted hair. The homeless Disney princess is back.

"Hello, Marta." Mr. L gets up and smiles. "Welcome back."

"I'm back *temporarily*." She narrows her eyes and announces it to the room. "Ya get it? I said *temporarily*."

"Good to have you back," Mr. L says carefully. "Temporarily."

The chatter begins.

"Class, quiet!" Mr. L yells. He's furious. "No more. Not a peep."

Marta picks up her roller backpack and drags it over as many toes as she can as she tries to cut through to her seat in the last row, next to Lillian. But before she can make it to the third row, I grab her arm and stop her. "Don't. Please, Marta. Sit next to me."

She practically spits on me. "I have my seat," she says, her eyes dead ahead on the empty seat next to Lillian. That's when someone sticks out their foot and Marta falls flat on her face in the middle of the room.

202

The whole class inhales. *"Ohhhh!"* But not a single person tries to help her. Marta looks at Lillian and Erica, but they just smack their gum and giggle like no one is lying on the floor in a puddle of shame, right in front of their faces.

I try to help, but Mr. Judgmental Bobby Brown pushes me out of the way and lifts her up like she doesn't weigh a thing. Marta doesn't look at me, but at least she doesn't punch me in the face. She takes her old seat next to me and slumps.

Mr. L resumes class, but all I can think about is the broken girl next to me, and I feel horrible.

QUESTION: Is it better to try and fail miserably than not try at all and never fail?

At snack, I look for her everywhere and finally find her in my favorite stall in the upstairs girls' bathroom. Her Crocs and socks give her away. "Marta?"

No answer. "I know you're in there."

"What do you want?"

"They're leaving in one hour for the JOs. I know we can get you on that flight if you just come out of the bathroom." She's quiet for a long time. "Marta?"

"They gave it to you, didn't they?" She sniffles and flushes the toilet.

"Yeah, they did." I brace myself against the sink. The door could fly open any second. "But here's the thing, Marta—" I'm about to launch into the whole explanation of how I didn't ask for it back. How I didn't even want it . . . when I hear her say in a voice I barely recognize but remember deeply:

"Take it." Sniffle, sniffle, huge snot blow.

Say what? I check out her feet just to make sure it's really her. Yep, Crocs. She hasn't moved. "What did you say?"

"You heard me."

"You mean . . ." I tread carefully. "It's okay with you if I take it?"

"No!" she yells. "I mean I *want* you to take it."

My heart beats harder. It all depended on this moment. Until I knew Marta was okay with it, I would not allow myself to consider it. But there's still one condition to my taking the job, and it's not negotiable. "I'll do it if you go to the JOs—"

"No." She cuts me off. "It's too late for me." The toilet flushes; she walks out. Her nose is so swollen it's double the size. "Coach will never allow me back on the team, and he's right."

"It's not too late." I tap my watch. But it would be soon. "Just go and apologize." I push her toward the sink. She sees herself in the mirror and starts to cry.

"All of you should hate me." She snorts. "I deserve everything I get. I'm an idiot, a sucker, a blind fool. I was mean, horrible, and conceited."

Pen would say that about me on a good day. "Yeah, yeah, me too. But it is over, all right?" I open the door and push her out into the hallway. "Water under the bridge." We walk all the way down the stairs. I've got my hand on her neck, pushing her forward. People are looking, but I don't care. When we get near the multi-purpose room I see Bobby shooting baskets. He stops and gives me this horrible look. "What are you doing to her now?"

I ignore him.

"It's a waste of time." Marta wipes her nose on her sleeve. "He'll never want me back."

From the corner of my eye I see Bobby dribbling toward us. I walk faster. I don't have time to deal with him right now.

"I'm such a total loser." Marta keeps up with the self-pity.

Before I can deliver a swift elbow to his face, Bobby pulls my hand off Marta. "What are you doing?"

I push him away and keep going until I get to the doors. I'm afraid if I let go, she's gonna go run and play in traffic or something dumb.

Bobby's back. "Let go of her, Coop." He acts like he's her bodyguard.

I kick the door open with my foot. "Marta's got a plane to catch, all right? So either get out of my way or hold the dang doors."

Bobby's so surprised, he drops his ball and it rolls away.

"Bobby." I point to the doors.

"Oh, okay, yeah, sure." He pushes them open. I feel Marta freeze. They're all there, the whole team getting ready for the biggest trip of their lives.

"Go, Marta!" Bobby tries to high-five her. But the minute her eyes land on Coach, I can feel her whole body go dead. He's in the middle of training the team. They're on the bars, the beam, and the mats. They look like a well-oiled machine in their team uniforms, beautiful and strong. Complete. And for the first time I get it—I see it from Lillian's perspective, even from Erica's. Marta did not belong. Marta was not a team player. Marta was an individual. On her own she was great, but as a member of the team, all she did was make them look bad. And for a second I actually feel bad for them. With her in the game, Coach would never care about them.

"Charlie, I'm scared." Marta backs away, totally terrorized. "I can't talk to him. No way. He'll spit in my face. I'd spit in my face."

I don't blame her. I'd be scared too. But this isn't the time to back down. Her destiny is too great. I believed that, just as I believed mine was possibly even greater.

Bobby pushes her forward. We hold the door open and keep Marta in the doorway until Coach sees her. And when he does, he stops yelling at the perfect trio of girls and walks over to her. Boy, does he look mad. Bobby and I make ourselves scarce.

"What do you want?" Coach yells, and everything stops. Suddenly all eyes are on Marta.

"Nothing." Marta's hands fly up. She turns to walk away.

"What did you say?" Coach yells after her.

She stops. "I'm sorry," she says. "I just wanted to say I'm sorry."

He rubs his giant belly. "Everyone is sorry. What does sorry mean? Without action, it means nothing." He points to the back wall, lined with suitcases and backpacks. "We are leaving in less than one hour—leaving without *you*, Marta Urloff."

Marta begins to cry. I gotta tell you—seeing Marta cry is enough to make just about the toughest criminal break down. Her whole body shakes. Her entire face crumbles. Snot pours out like a geyser.

It works like a charm on Coach. Within minutes, he throws his arms around her like a giant bear and goes off in a stream of Russian I'm not sure even Marta understands.

Lillian, Erica, and Lola are watching from across the gym. Their mouths open, their bodies hunched. "Yeah, you lost," I mouth into the air. I love it.

Meanwhile Marta pulls out of his embrace. Her face is covered in snot and convoluted in tears. "I have brought disgrace on you, on the country, and worst of all, on my mother's name." She bounces her head against his chest "I was lured by Hollywood. I feel sick at my stupidity."

His huge hand rubs her back. "People fall for it all the time. Look at your friend there." He points right at me.

"Charlie. Of course Charlie falls for it." She wipes her eyes. "But me, Marta Urloff?"

"Nice, huh?" Bobby nudges me and laughs.

But I know Marta. It means she loves me again.

Coach pulls her away and looks into her eyes. "Never lose sight of the gold medal. You, Marta Urloff, daughter of the great Olga Cochenko, are the only one here who will go all the way."

The team's faces drop.

He raises her hand like a champion, even though right now she looks nothing like one. She looks horrible, but at least she looks like her old self. "This weekend you will come, you will qualify for the Elites, and you will blow the world of gymnastics away. This is only the beginning."

"You will not be disappointed." She wipes her face.

Coach picks up his clipboard. "Bus is leaving in twenty-five minutes for airport. I will talk to Pickler and call your aunt." He shakes his head. "She is crazy, that lady."

And then suddenly Marta goes white. "But I don't have my stuff. Coach. I can't go. It will take too long for my aunt to get here—"

He waves his hand high. "Lillian, Erica, and Lola," he snaps at them. They glare from the beam. "You will share your luggage with Marta, won't you?"

They stare at him like he's speaking Chinese. "What?" Lillian frowns.

Erica puts both her hands to her ears. "Excuse me?"

"Share luggage?" Lola says, horrified.

"I said"—Coach's voice gets louder, rougher—"your teammate needs to borrow some of your gear." He zeroes in on

Lillian. "As captain, you understand?"

This is like watching the bad guy drop to his knees. Poetry.

"You want *me* to share my clothes? With, with . . . Marta?" She can barely get the words out.

"Yes," he says. "I do. It's only for a few days. I have her team leotard in my office. So it's just clothes."

"Just clothes. Just my clothes." Lillian bites her lip. She looks like she's about to throw up.

Erica watches the situation and sees her opportunity. She pushes Lillian aside and runs over. "I'll share my clothes, Coach. Of course I'll share my clothes."

Marta shakes her head. "What a bunch of phonies."

"No, no, I'm sharing my clothes. No one wants your clothes. They want mine." Lillian pushes Erica aside. "I will share, Coach."

"My stuff will totally fit her." Lola waves her hand high in the air.

I hope Marta pees and farts in every last leotard she borrows. I touch Marta's arm lightly. "Good luck."

Marta looks at me. It's a while before she speaks. "Who would have thought we'd come so far so fast?"

"It's only November," I say. "You're heading to the JOs—"

Marta cuts me off. "And you're heading to Hollywood."

Bobby gives me a dirty look, shakes his head. "I told her it was lame to take your job—"

"What's lame is her *not* taking it." Marta grabs both my

209

shoulders in her usual manner and yells in my face. "If you don't take it, I swear I'm coming after you. You hear me?"

"Wait a sec—" Bobby's face suddenly changes. "So you didn't already take it?"

"No, you jerk." I hit him.

"She said no until I said yes." Marta grabs Bobby's sleeve. "You'd better make her call Chad today. Make her take it."

"So on the bus, you hadn't—" Bobby drops his head. "I feel like a real jerk."

"Yeah, well, you are." I punch him on the arm.

"Yo!" Lillian yells. "Marta, come on!"

Marta turns and waves. "Take Hollywood by storm. I'm going for gold." Marta runs over to a mat and starts stretching. She's finally back where she belongs.

As I watch her, I feel like a huge weight has been lifted from my shoulders.

"I'm such a jerk," Bobby says. "Don't ever trust me again."

"I won't." I start walking away.

"Hey." Bobby runs after me. "So are you taking it?"

"Maybe."

We're about halfway up the stairs when Pen comes running past. She's got her posters under her arms. She stops, out of breath. "Did you hear we won?"

"Won what?" Bobby checks out her poster of a flattened owl. "That's nasty."

"Tell me about it. They're all over my room. Every time I open my eyes, I'm looking at roadkill."

"Not roadkill. Lives, Charlie. They're lives." The bell rings. Pen sees everyone beginning to scatter. "The city came back this morning and said the builders have to make a path behind those nasty capitalist eyesores so the animals can walk through. We won."

Yes! I can't believe it. I throw her a high five. "You actually beat the Skips of this world?"

Pen looks about as shocked as I do. "I couldn't believe it either. It's going into law the first of January. They're going to have to clear the construction out of the corridor and move their dumb Bentleys so the animals have room to walk."

"This place is historic," Bobby says, and I know he means it. "It should be protected."

"Just you wait. We've got some big things in the works." Pen gets that look of total determination I know so well.

TRUE FACT: My sister actually made a difference in the world.

The team starts marching out of the MPR. All of them with their bags. Pen turns. "They're leaving for the JOs now?" She looks sad.

I point. "Keep looking."

Finally Marta comes out. She's last, of course, has no bags, but with Coach's arm around her she looks like a star. She waves at me and yells, "See you on TV!"

When Pen sees Marta, her face explodes. "She's going? You got her to go!"

Bobby looks so proud.

"Well done. I knew you could do it." The second bell rings. "All right, people, I gotta go." Pen runs off toward the high school, and Bobby and I walk up the next set of stairs.

When we get to the top, I'm huffing and puffing. Kids are swarming, trying to push past us. But Bobby is calm and collected. He pulls open the door. We walk down the hallway toward class. We're all alone. Just before we get to Mr. L's door, Bobby stops and asks, "You ever been to the Country Store for ice cream after school?"

Butterfly alert! They're swarming all over me. The more he looks at me, the more my entire stomach feels like I'm about to launch down a Six Flags roller coaster. "Uh." I swallow. "Nope."

"Would you like to?" He's so close I can smell his breath. It's like warm purple grapes. Yep, purple. "With me, maybe?"

"Um, yeah, I'd—" And then out of the blue he leans in and kisses me ON THE LIPS!!!!

TRUE FACT: I've practiced in the mirror, but don't ever, and I mean ever, repeat that.

212

My first kiss.

Thank God no one was in the hallway.

Thank the spirits above my lips were closed.

Thank Krishna they were covered in my MAC Rock and Roll red that I'd blotted to give me that stained look that doesn't wear off. But most of all, thank Buddha for Trident Spearmint gum.

When he pulls back, he opens his eyes and looks right at me. "That was nice."

Nice? It was holy! Supernatural. Goose bumps fire up all over my skin. Sweat trickles down my back. My heart is beating so hard I feel like puking. "Yeah, not bad." I run for the bathroom.

"Yo!" Bobby yells after me. "So is it a date?"

"I'll see if I can fit you in." I push open the bathroom door and collapse against the cold tile wall. The final bell rings. Who the heck needs Hollywood? I just kissed Mr. Bobby Brown.

Acknowledgments

My lovely editor Alyson Day—you have been such a pleasure to work with. Thank you for your endless patience and your supremely upbeat personality, which makes the process of shredding a manuscript to pieces a little less painful. To Toni Markiet, for being so generous with her expert eye.

To Tom Forget and Amy Ryan—what can I say? You two are the masters at getting Charlie and her vibe just right. You're brilliant.

To Renée Cafiero, copyeditor extraordinaire, thank you for making me look more literate than I am.

And a special thanks to Olivia deLeon and Jenna Lisanti for doing so much to get Charlie into the hands of children and parents, teachers and librarians.

Finally, to my agent, Victoria Sanders: you're one of a kind. Thank you for coming to the rescue when I really need it.

Meet Charlie C. Cooper,

so-called middle child, who must face down the mean girls to uncover the meaning of true friendship.

Maria T. Lennon

Confessions OF A So-called Middle Child

See how Charlie's story began!

HARPER

An Imprint of HarperCollinsPublishers

www.harpercollinschildrens.com